For The Sake Of Art

By

Michelle Hockley

All characters in this novella are fictitious and are not based
on real people.

Front Cover:
Equanimity (Acrylic on canvas) by Michelle Hockley

To the special people in my life
Mum, Dad, Anita and Ian

And my reader

CHAPTER ONE

The Flower Girl

Peter Dowling drums his fingers in a light, regular beat as he waits for someone to take his statement. He isn't nervous, but the unfamiliar surroundings are causing him much discomfort, not least by the one-way mirror that stares out in a sinister, Cold War, under the spotlight sort of way. The fluorescent strip light, with an incessant hum, and the dark grey dowdy walls, are enough to convince Peter that the décor alone, would steer anyone from a life of crime. A dusty tape recorder on the desk is switched off. Peter imagines the many hundreds of interviews conducted in this room: a world completely unknown to Mr Dowling and if she hadn't disappeared, it would have stayed that way.

Every other Thursday, since his retirement four months ago, he'd seen her selling flowers in the market at the far right corner, adjacent to Pimlico square, Chelsea. Yet, for the last two weeks, when he was ready to make contact, she was missing. This morning, Peter took matters into his own hands and decided to report this anomaly. A procedure he'd expected would be straightforward; simply giving details to a member of staff at the front desk.

The brown Bakelite clock on the wall shows just after mid-day. Peter contemplates lunch, seeing himself standing before an open refrigerator in his kitchen, choosing a fine pâté on wholemeal bread accompanied by one of the choice chutneys from *Partridges* on the King's Road. Otherwise, at this time, he'd be scouring the archives of a gallery or auction room unearthing the whereabouts of an elusive object d'art for the clients of his old chum, Cedric Carlton-Smyth; an art dealer at *Drakes*, the Auctioneers. Peter has known Cedric since way back when they were both reading History at Oxford and despite their personalities being polar opposites, they have, in recent times, formed a surprisingly workable partnership. Carlton-Smyth is never happier than when fully immersed in the world of glamour; rubbing shoulders with the rich, helping them to fulfil their high cultured desires to locate a unique piece of art. Whilst Peter on the other hand loves nothing more than being absorbed in documents, delving into the whereabouts of a piece of art and checking its provenance. A partnership that is very much enhanced by Peter's splendid reputation as a researcher, gained whilst Senior Record Specialist at *The British Archives*. He never failed to find that one nugget of information to make a difficult subject of the past attainable; all be it sometimes at the eleventh hour. With credentials such as these, he is very useful to Cedric Carlton-Smyth.

In the interview room next to where Peter continues to wait, Detective Constable Sarah Henderson is reaching the end of a long and trying interrogation. Detective Constable Gilmore enters the room requesting her to take a statement for a missing person.

'Okay,' replies Sarah Henderson, 'I'll be there in five,' she adds, keen to oblige, not wanting to ruffle any more feathers, having not yet completed her probation. Landing this new role so soon after joining Blythe Street Police Station here in Chelsea, London, was as much a surprise to her as begrudging to her colleagues; causing a good deal of friction between her and her peers. It was Detective Chief Inspector Malcolm Monroe, a long-standing member of Blythe Street, some 30 years and nearing retirement, who'd suggested she apply and he pretty much groomed her to pass the interview. His encouragement gave Sarah Henderson the confidence to submit an application and quite frankly, any thought of her backing out was never an option after the effort Monroe had made to school her.

As she marks up the tape recordings and tidies her papers to close another arduous interview, doubts about her ability surface and a flood of insecurities and irritations make themselves known. *A missing person report?* she thinks. *What a blooming cheek. That's the job of a junior at front desk not a DC. So that's another meal I shall miss, which Monroe won't, evident by the size of his girth.* She tries to suppress the notion that she's been given this menial task because Monroe has lost respect for her achievements and that Human Resources have already put the wheels in motion for her demotion. Yet, negative thoughts win out and the chiding of herself continues. *If the missing person,* she thinks, *is not at the very least, Prince Harry, then it's quite possible, a P45 is already in the post.*

When Sarah joined the force it was the research that attracted her; happy to spend any amount of time rummaging through old case files; reassuring the team that no stone had been left unturned. With limitless amounts of patience it was a pleasure for her to watch hours upon hours of CCTV footage to learn the movements of a suspect. Whereas in her role as a DC, although she relishes the challenge, it's becoming increasingly apparent to Sarah that this role requires a different set of skills to those where she had previously excelled. What's more, she's finding it difficult to fit in with her new unit, not least because she landed this role, but more so it's her temperament, unable to relate to her colleagues who often josh and prank to let off steam from the horrendous scenes they encounter everyday. Since DC Henderson doesn't socialise with the department, she has never come to understand their quirks. In fact, the only person whose path she has crossed outside of work, is DCI Monroe. A chance meeting, just prior to her interview, along Brick Lane, in the East End of London, not far from her flat. Since Monroe seemed to be hovering in the vicinity of her front door, she felt obliged to invite him inside for coffee where Monroe immediately lost himself in her CD and DVD collection; commenting on her eclectic taste.

Detective Henderson closes the door on her interview. DC Gilmore hands her a brown A4 paper file. 'Sorry Henderson,' he says. 'They are up to their eyes on the front desk. The bloody bag snatcher's back on the King's Road. I hope you don't mind.' Before she has a chance to say anything, she glances down at the title written in bold black letters, and is immediately taken aback.

Mr P. Dowling
A Missing Person Report

Peter Dowling looks up from the floor on hearing the interview room door unlatch; anticipating the arrival of coffee; a notion quickly replaced by one of shock.

'Sarah Henderson. Oh my goodness, it's you Sarah. What a surprise. How are you?' says Peter, half rising from his seat.

Henderson's heart sinks at the realisation that it is indeed the same Mr Dowling, but remaining the ever professional, she pulls out the wooden chair from beneath the desk, places the brown A4 file on the table and without making eye contact, addresses Mr Dowling with determined authority. She is fully aware that if Mr Dowling was here as a criminal or a victim, she'd be expected, under Blythe Street policy, to inform Monroe of her acquaintance. But since this is neither the case, she's confident to proceed with the interview.

'Good afternoon Mr Dowling,' begins Sarah. 'This will not take long.'

'Sarah. Don't you remember me?' interrupts Peter, leaning closer into the table, changing his tone to a whisper. 'I'm so relieved to see a familiar face. This long wait has caused me to feel quite queasy.'

Sarah pushes further back into her chair trying to regain an equilibrium of presence, whilst praying for a sinkhole to appear directly under her desk. She inhales deeply to control her emotions as her stomach somersaults and her neck reddens because ten years ago, on leaving her post as researcher at *The British Archives,* she'd hoped that would be the last she'd encounter the likes of Peter Dowling. Having now no choice but to proceed with the interview, she opens the brown A4 file and reads out the first question from the form.

'Mr Dowling, can I take your address, please?' Their domestic arrangements had never arisen in any previous conversation. In fact, prior to *The British Archives*' Christmas party, where they'd spent most of the evening entwined in each others' arms, their focus had always been very much on their work; predominately completing a project allocated to them by the Foreign and Commonwealth team.

Sarah's toes clench inside her sensible low-heeled court shoes as she recalls those uncharacteristic images of herself being wrapped in Peter's arms; slobbering over each other for the best part of the evening. She feels her face grimace at the mere indignity she must have displayed that evening and clears her throat to restore her attention back to the present; taking note of the next question on the investigation form.

'Thank you Mr Dowling. I now require the name of the missing person please?'

'I'm sorry, I don't have a name,' replies Dowling.

'Oh,' says Sarah, firmly halted in her tracks; pen hovering over the form.

'I don't know her name, but I know she is the flower seller on the Pimlico Market. You know the market, it's on an island, practically in the middle of the road.'

'Then can you give me a description of the girl, a photograph if you have one?'

'A photograph?' barks Peter. 'How rude of you to suggest such a thing. What do you take me for? A pervert? A photograph of a member of the public,' protests Peter as he fidgets uncomfortably in his seat.

Michelle Hockley

'I didn't mean. Oh never mind,' says DC Henderson, somewhat flabbergasted whilst at the same time desperately trying to keep her cool. 'Do you have, at the very least, a description? Something from memory, anything Mr Dowling, please? What about the person's age? Can we start with her age?'

'I'm not very good with ages,' Peter replies.

Holy Moses, thinks Sarah. *This has got to be a joke*; scanning the room for Jeremy Beadle before remembering he's been long dead.

'If you push me for an age of this woman,' starts Peter, 'I'd say about 35 years old.'

Then, in one breath, Dowling begins to reel off a description.

'She's very pretty. Olive skin. Tall. Very long legs. A brunette I think. Yes, that's right a brunette. In fact, a very shiny brunette and slim in build.'

'Okay,' replies Sarah, after recording the details of a woman we might all aspire to be.

'Does that help?' asks Peter.

'Yes, and thank you for your time Mr Dowling. I shall have these details circulated to the relevant officers at all seaports and airports.'

Sarah rustles her papers back into the brown A4 folder and makes her way to the door leaving no doubt that the meeting has terminated. Quick to recognise the signs, Peter stands up and pushes his chair back beneath the table with the utmost precision. After taking one final glance at the room that may once have heard details of the most damaging of crimes, he follows Sarah to the front desk.

Standing alone outside on the concrete steps of the station, Peter embraces the familiar sound of buses as they thunder along Sloane Avenue. He takes a moment to button his long grey overcoat before putting on his leather gloves and positioning his trilby firmly on his head. Acknowledging the need to clear his mind, he doesn't hail a taxicab, instead begins to plan his route home to Cheyne Walk via; Cale Street, then down to the King's Road and south along Chelsea Manor Street towards the River Thames. As he gets into his stride, it isn't long before the customary sounds of London start to mute and be replaced by his thoughts. First to sweep into his mind is Sarah Henderson and that Christmas party. He'd understood many years ago that it had been a mistake for Sarah. She'd made that quite clear when sending him to *Coventry* on her return from New Year. Though it was puzzling to Peter why anyone would hold negative thoughts for a decade; concluding that her aloofness and coldness towards him was simply borne out of a professionalism towards the Metropolitan Police. 'Hmm,' he says to himself, agreeing to put that particular conundrum to bed to make room for another thought to enter his mind space as he continues to stride out at a reasonable pace. This time, that of the flower girl who is no longer on the Pimlico Market. He feels reasonably comfortable for having alerted the police to a missing person, but is left with an awful nagging worry of having inadvertently perverted the course of justice by being too economical with the truth. As he mulls over what offence he might have committed, he's distracted by aromas of the Mediterranean permeating from the Bistro on the corner of Cheyne Row. With his nose instinctively drawn towards a bouquet of garlic, fresh basil and a dashing of olive oil, any doubts he might be harbouring quickly dissipate in favour of lunch. Turning into Cheyne Walk his gait quickens towards the steps of his white terraced town house leading up to the front door. With a lightness of step he takes two at a time, smiling as he finds his key and unlocks the door.

Glancing at his watch, Peter knows that Ella, his cleaning lady, will have finished for the day, but out of politeness calls to let her know he has returned. As expected, he receives no reply and proceeds with putting his keys and gloves into the antique bowl on the mahogany hall table and placing his hat and coat on the stand opposite the staircase. A sense of normality begins to return; confirmed by the joys of home comforts as he slips off his brogues and slides his feet effortlessly into the soft leather of his moccasin slippers. Seeing The Daily Telegraph folded neatly on the side, he picks it up and makes his way to the sitting room.

'Hello Peter', says Anna-Belle, whose long legs, accentuated by black knee length suede boots over tight black jeans are crossed confidently over Mr Dowling's cream sofa. Her shiny brunette hair tied in a ponytail makes way for the black turtle neck beneath a black leather jacket that creaks to the rhythm of her inflated ego. With one arm flung over the back of the sofa and the other resting on an over sized plump, gold threaded embossed cushion, this cameo is perfectly framed and is complete.

Peter grips the newspaper tightly against his ribs trying to gain stability from a cold sensation rushing through his entire body.

'Oh my goodness,' he says nervously, 'you're the flower girl.'

'Well, well, well. So, you're Mr Dowling. Tut Tut, Mr Dowling you missed your delivery deadline. You are a bad boy to expect me to come to you and collect the package.'

'You're in my house. How dare you break into my house,' replies Peter, upset to the point of wanting to burst into tears.

'Calm down, Sonny Jim. Your cleaning lady let me wait for you. Though she didn't know you had a niece.'

'That's because I don't have a niece,' growls Peter

out of pure frustration.

'Blah Blah. Whatever, Mr Dowling.'

'I've been to the police today,' starts Peter. 'I reported you missing.'

'You've done what?' screeches Anna-Belle. 'You ridiculous man. What did you do that for? You utter fool.'

'Because Cedric Carlton-Smyth gave me strict instructions whilst he was away, to deliver the object d'art I'd been asked to collect, to you on the Pimlico Market. He never makes a mistake on my deliveries. What was I meant to do?'

'Well not that,' replies Anna-Belle. 'How can any of what you've just said make sense to you? Are you actually saying that when you thought to contact the police it seemed like the most sensible solution?'

'Yes. You were missing and I was genuinely concerned,' replies Peter.

'Jeeze,' blurts Anna-Belle, crossing her arms reaffirming her superiority.

'I didn't give your name,' adds Peter. 'I don't even know your name. I did tell them you had a flower stall on the Pimlico Market.'

'Well that is even more insane. The police will definitely have your card marked as the Chelsea idiot.'

Peter makes a beeline for the telephone on the table behind the standard lamp; surprising himself that his legs still work, having not felt them since he walked into the sitting room.

'I'm telephoning Mr Carlton-Smyth, right away.'

'Good luck with that,' replies Anna-Belle as she watches him move with added determination.

'I'm going to try anyway. And why don't they have a mobile signal in the Serengeti?'

'In the where?' asks Anna-Belle.

'The Serengeti. You know, Africa. He's currently on safari. That much I do know.'

'Is that what he told you? Oh you really are a fool.'

'Well, at least I'm not trespassing or breaking and entering a private property,' Peter replies holding the telephone receiver closer to his eyes; squinting as he looks for the redial button.

The front door knocker strikes three times, 'bang, bang, bang,' echoing inside the hallway; filtering inside the sitting room.

'Its the door,' shouts Anna-Belle, looking at Peter Dowling who is fully focused on the telephone.

'Oh for goodness sake who can that be?' mutters Peter, toying between making the call or answering the door.

'Leave the door,' shouts Anna-Belle, irritated by the continual delay of her collecting Peter's delivery. 'It will only be Jehovah Witnesses or born again Christians trying to convert your faith.'

On hearing such a derogatory comment about another person's religion, Dowling makes the decision to put down the receiver and deal with the door.

'No Mr Dowling. Just get the package so I can get out of your hair.'

'How dare you tell me to whom I can and cannot open my own front door. How dare you young lady.'

'Ooh la la. Young lady? Oh I like that,' she calls, flicking her toe from her crossed legs, slightly embarrassed that Mr Dowling had the gall to delay on her demands.

Peter throws the newspaper down on the hall table giving him both hands free to unlatch the door.

'Hello Mr Dowling. I'm DC Sarah Henderson,' she says holding up her badge. 'I've come with an update on your missing person. Do you have a moment please?'

'Er...yes. Yes of course come on through to the study,' replies Peter, closing the door as Sarah hovers at the threshold of the sitting room.

'Oh, I am so sorry Mr Dowling, you have company. Would you rather I come back another time?'

With a confident smile, Anna-Belle rises to her feet and moves forward to shake Sarah's hand. 'Hello, I'm Anna-Belle, Peter's niece.'

'Hello, pleased to meet you Anna-Belle,' replies Sarah, shaking hands.

Peter falls in line, going along with Anna-Belle's story of being his niece, choosing not to muddy the waters of an already complicated situation; even though he recognises this as an opportunity to inform the police of having an intruder in his house. Instead, he offers DC Henderson privacy by leading her out of the sitting room, down the hallway.

On entering the study, Sarah is at once struck by the richly embossed carpet and splendid décor that frames the many shelves of books from floor to ceiling. Without sitting down, for fear of damaging the delicate silks on the salon chairs, Sarah gets straight to the purpose of her visit.

'Mr Dowling, I have made some progress with your enquiry and wanted to include you in my early findings.'

'Please do go ahead,' replies Peter, thinking, *this should be interesting*.

'I have to admit, I became curious with what you reported to Blythe Street Station today. So, on my way to buy a late lunch, I checked out the Pimlico Market and you are quite right Mr Dowling.'

'Am I?'

'You are indeed, for there is a flower stall,' Sarah explains.

'But no flower girl,' adds Peter.

'Oh yes, there is a flower lady at the flower stall

but she doesn't fit the description you have given. I was wondering, therefore, if the information you've submitted is quite as accurate as it could be?'

'Yes, it's as accurate as I can provide,' replies Peter unable to suppress a slightly sarcastic tone, given that the description he has given is currently occupying the sofa in his sitting room.

'Do you wish to add anything to your report, Mr Dowling?'

Peter wanted more than anything to explain about the intruder, about the niece he doesn't have and the package he should have given to the flower girl. He no longer wishes to carry this burden and after wrestling with his options, decides to tell everything and bear the consequences of whatever comes with wasting police time.

'Well,' starts Peter thoughtfully, 'I did perhaps...' stuttering as he tries to find the right words.

'Go on Mr Dowling,' says Sarah, moving from one foot to the other, taking out a notebook from her pocket.

On seeing a police officer standing in front of him with notebook and pencil poised, Peter instantly loses his pluck to explain and instead, takes a different route to shut down this drama.

'Okay, I was a little hasty in my coming to the police and I apologise for wasting your time. I hope there won't be any fallout from my actions.'

'But Mr Dowling', says Sarah.

'Oh, please, Sarah, call me Peter.'

'Mr Dowling,' repeats Sarah. 'You are an intelligent man and your decision to bring your concerns to the police station would not have been made on a whim. Thus, it's impossible for me to overlook what you've reported. I shall therefore, ask you again to enlighten me further on what you know with regard to this missing woman?'

The moment she expels these words, Peter witnesses the penny in her mind drop.

'Anna-Belle', says Sarah, pointing in the direction of the sitting room. 'She's the missing person. Your niece is the missing person? Why did you allow me to go on? Why didn't you call the station to let us know your niece had been found.'

'She's not my...' starts Peter, until halted by a staggeringly loud knock on the back door, causing him to literally jump and squeal as he turns to face the study door. A series of heavy thumps follow, causing Peter to call out, hoping, if nothing else, to save the paintwork from being chipped. 'I'm coming. Coming,' he calls in a pitch almost reaching falsetto; rushing through to the kitchen.

Behind the half drawn Roman blind, used to obscure the clear glazed back door; having so far resisted the idea of installing iron bars like his neighbours, he can just make out the bellowing of cream coloured cloth from two dresses.

'It's my friends, Margo and Cassandra, the two lovely sisters from number 24,' he shouts excitedly over his left shoulder keeping DC Sarah Henderson in the loop, conscious that she's waiting for his explanation. 'I won't be long,' he adds.

'You carry on,' replies Sarah, scrambling for the telephone number in her phone so she can retract the need for all sea and airports to maintain a watchful eye for the missing person's description she gave them.

Peter calls out to his visitors as he stretches up and bends down to release the locks situated along the length of the door. 'My you two are in a hurry. Is it an emergency Margo? What's wrong with the front door today, ladies?' he asks, until, finally releasing the last bolt, throwing open the door with a flourish. 'Oh. I do apologise gentlemen. I thought it was...'

In a strong Moroccan accent, 'Good Afternoon, we are here to take you to the airport,' says one of the more portly gentlemen dressed from head to toe in Arab garb.

'Oh, I do apologise again gentlemen. You appear to have the wrong address. Have you tried the house next door?'

'No, Mr Dowling, it's you we are here to collect. '

'Oh my good Lord, you know my name,' says Peter, holding a clenched hand to his mouth.

'We have instructions to take you to the airport.'

'But I've already said, I'm not going to the airport today. Good day to you both. Good bye Gentlemen,' closing the door as he speaks, not wishing to appear rude.

Before the door has a chance to latch, it swings back open with such a force, banging against the kitchen wall, knocking Peter off balance.

'Is everything okay in there?' shouts Sarah.

Peter opens his mouth to reply to her, but nothing comes out. The two gentlemen, standing side by side almost the width of the kitchen and towering over Peter, indicate for Peter to close the door that leads to the hallway. Fully co-operating, daring only to do what he is instructed, closes the door to give the gentlemen his full attention.

Meanwhile, Anna-Belle, still in the sitting room and long since lost the last of her patience, takes out her phone.

'About bloody time,' replies Detective Chief Inspector Malcolm Monroe. 'Where are you? What is going on?'

'I'm in the house of that very weird Peter Dowling,' she replies in a whisper.

'What exactly are you doing there Detective

Sergeant Anna-Belle Trait?'

'What do you think? Collecting the outstanding object d'art that Dowling should have delivered two weeks ago. Only I can't, because that idiot Henderson has turned up delaying me.'

'What's she doing there?' asks Monroe

'Shush. I can hear blokes talking in the kitchen. Strong Arab accents. Who have you sent now?'

'No one. I didn't send Henderson either. What's she doing there?'

'Following up on a missing person investigation that was reported to Blythe Street nick by that dick-head Dowling.'

'What? Who's he lost? His way? Or Carlton-Smyth?' sniggers Monroe.

'No. Me?'

'You? Well he's found you now. Did Henderson see you?'

'Yes, I shook hands. I've no idea what description Dowling gave to your nick, but she couldn't find me and I stood right in front of her. Stupid bitch. I told you she was useless.'

'She's perfect for what we need. She'll have her uses because she's useless. We can lay anything at her door, she'd never notice.'

'She's a liability. I've told you before, and I'm telling you again.'

'Well, you're not so perfect yourself. Where have you been these past two weeks? Why were you not on your mark at the market?'

'No time for explanations now Monroe. What is my next move?'

'I need you to get your hands on that package. What a bloody mess this is turning out to be.'

'Shush,' whispers Anna-belle. Those blokes are still here. There's some commotion coming from the back of the house. I think that's Henderson's voice.'

In the study, the more slender of the two Arabs drags Sarah on to the chair behind the desk and yanks free, the curtain tie-back to throw around her waist as she fumbles in her pocket to look for her badge.

'Stop. Metropolitan Police. You are under arrest,' says Sarah Henderson failing to realise her position of authority is making zero impact.

The second tie-back rips from the curtain and is slung around her mouth from where nothing more than an incoherent muffle can be heard. The stout Arab appears on the threshold of the open study door holding Mr Dowling firmly in an armlock. Peter peers into the room, eyes wide and shaking like a frozen cat as the gun presses further and further into the nape of his neck. Sweat drips down his forehead as he watches the thin Arab ransack his desk; opening every drawer, removing paper files and an A-Z of London, until a small package is found and held aloft towards the other Arab in a triumphant explosion. Peter's hopes of an early release, now the package has been found, are soon dashed. The pushing and shoving starts over. This time, down the hallway towards the front door.

Anna-Belle, having heard what she described to Monroe as commotion, sees Peter going past the sitting room door. The gun momentarily leaving Peter's spine to take aim in Anna-Belle's direction.

'La tataharak. La tataharak,' shouts the more stout Arab. Don't move. Don't move.

'La tatliquu alnaar,' replies Anna-Belle. Don't shoot, as a bullet leaves the gun at speed, hitting the painting hanging on the wall, just above her head.

'La tatliquu alnaar,' she repeats, buckling down, grabbing an antique foot-stall to hold against her as a shield.

At the sound of gunshot Peter shrieks and collapses to the floor like an abandoned stringed puppet. He lets out an extended groan on being dragged up to his feet and the muzzle of the gun being returned to his back; pushing ever further into his skeleton. Peter freezes with fear when the front door is opened; exiting only after being thrust with force to leave his home. His toes scrape and bounce down the stone steps before being flung into the back seat of a stately, black, polished car, accompanied by one of his captors. As the car pulls slowly away, the second Arab slams shut Peter Dowling's front door and in triple time he runs down the steps leaping inside the moving vehicle. All four car doors click and are centrally locked.

'Adhhab. Adhhab, Heliport. Adhhab.' Go. Go, Heliport. Go.

Hearing the front door slam shut, Anna-Belle Trait begins to unfurl from her temporary barricade.

'Trait. Trait,' shouts Monroe trying to be heard on the still open line now halfway slung under the sofa. 'What's going on? Speak to me and that's an order DS Trait.'

'Crikey, that was close,' says Trait, shaking her head. 'They've taken Dowling,' she adds.

'Who has. Who has taken him?'

'Two Arabs.'

'Where have they taken him? Have they got Henderson.'

'Don't know. Don't think so,' replies Trait, feeling somewhat dazed with the bullet fire still ringing in her ears.

'Go and look for her then. Let's hope a bullet didn't find its way to her,' says Monroe.

'Okay I'm onto it. Get a squad car to look for Dowling and the two Arabs. They can't have gone far, they've only just left,' replies Anna-Belle.

'You don't need to tell me how to do my job,'

retorts Monroe. 'Wheels are already in motion; the lads are on the streets.'

'Glad to hear it,' replies Trait.

'Trait. Listen. If you find Henderson alive, send her back to the station. We'll find her some paperwork to look at, she's safer with paper.'

'What do you want me to do, Monroe?'

'Carry on looking for that bloody package and then remind me never to involve you in my operations again.'

'Don't make me laugh. You forget Monroe, you've no choice but to keep me in; you're in way too deep on this one,' replies Anna-Belle as she walks down the hallway and enters the study.

Finding Henderson alive, Anna-Belle takes a penknife from inside her leather jacket and begins to cut away the curtain cord that is gagging Sarah.

'We'll have you out of here in no time DC Henderson,' says Anna-Belle.

'Mmm. Mmm,' replies Henderson, trying to form words before the cord falls away.

'DS Trait,' shouts Monroe from the open phone line now placed in Anna-Belle's back trouser pocket. 'Is she okay?'

'Yes, she's fine, Monroe. A little worse for wear, but she'll live, won't you Henderson?' says DS Trait.

Henderson splutters and shakes her head loose;

grappling to make sense of what she's hearing coming from the phone. 'Is that DCI Monroe I can hear? Monroe, from Blythe Street Police Station?' she says.

'Yes, that's right Henderson,' replies Trait, pushing Sarah forward to untie the cord around her waist.

'So, if you don't mind my asking,' says Henderson, staring up at Trait from the salon chair behind the desk. 'Who are you?'

'I don't mind you asking Henderson. I'm DS Anna-Belle Trait, Covert Operations with the Met police. Is that enough information for you?' replies Trait.

Sarah cocks her head to one side, furrows her brow creating a confused visage that can only have the desired effect of irritating Trait to distraction. 'Oh but...and...Mr Dowling's niece and the flower stall holder, is that correct?'

'Don't worry yourself Henderson,' snaps Trait as she continues to grapple with the knot in the cord before finally freeing Henderson from the curtain ties. 'If I was you,' continues Trait, 'I'd take the rest of the day off. Isn't that right Monroe?' she shouts to the phone, now slung across the desk, hoping for a resolve to remove the encumbrance that is Henderson.

'No,' shouts Henderson, rubbing her wrists; trying to regain some feeling. 'We have to find Mr Dowling quickly. If he's not already dead then he's in real danger. Those men came in here holding him at gun point whilst they searched Mr Dowling's desk. I thought they were going to kill him and I couldn't do anything to stop them. I heard a gunshot before they slammed the door and if they didn't get you,' says Henderson, looking at Trait, 'then did they shoot Dowling?' she says, starting slightly, to lose control of her emotions. 'I couldn't do anything Monroe, I was held up in this chair.'

'Monroe here,' he shouts. 'Listen, Henderson, can you hear me?'

'Yes, DCI Monroe,' replies Sarah, 'I can hear you,' picking up the mobile phone to her ear.

'Listen carefully, Henderson. Did the intruders find anything?'

'Yes, a small package or packet, whatever you'd like to call it. Wrapped in brown paper.'

'Okay, that is helpful Henderson. Now think Henderson. Did they take the package?'

'Yes and they've taken Mr Dowling,' she shouts. 'Why take him? They've surely got what they came for.'

'Calm down Henderson,' says Anna-Belle, confirming her earlier thoughts, that Monroe had made a mistake in making her a DC.

'Put the phone back on the desk Henderson,' instructs Monroe, to which she duly obliges, recognising from his tone, that she has just gone above her pay grade.

Art For Art's Sake

'At least try and calm down,' calls out Trait. 'I get that it's a big day for you Henderson, but let's save the drama for someone who might appreciate it, like someone at the Oscars.'

'My goodness you are rude,' replies Sarah Henderson. 'Whoever you might be; niece, flower girl, detective. Either way, you are incredibly rude.'

'Well, lets have less of the whining, because Monroe's got his finest on the streets of London looking for Mr Dowling. He has cars on the road as we speak and we shall just have to wait.'

'A car is no good,' shouts Henderson. 'They are going to the airport. I heard them at the backdoor when they arrived.'

'Airport?' repeats Trait.

'Yes. Airport,' says Sarah.

'Why didn't you say? Did you get that Monroe,' says Trait.

'Roger that,' says Monroe.

Anna-Belle immediately feels rage boiling on learning crucial information has not been acted upon. Without thinking, she grabs the lapels of Sarah's jacket tugging hard, 'which airport, Henderson? Quick, which airport?'

'I didn't hear them say which airport,' replies Sarah, pulling herself away from Trait's hold. 'And you don't need to be so rough. After all, you are supposed to be a girl.'

'Careful Henderson. If I had time, I'd give you a piece of my mind with that sexist comment.'

Ignoring Trait, Henderson leans towards the phone and shouts, 'wait Monroe, you need to notify Anti Kidnap and Extortion Unit. This is big.'

CHAPTER TWO

All Systems Go

The Bentley drives silently over Battersea Bridge before entering the heliport to come gracefully to a halt at a waiting helicopter. The gun, pressing firmly into Peter's ribs, is a permanent reminder that his life hangs by a thread as to whether his captor chooses to pull the trigger or not.

'Bsre,' quickly, shouts the more stout of the two Arabs, who has since responded to the name, Kassri. The car door flings open automatically. A yank on Peter's arm pulls him out from the back seat while the sinews in his armpit fall just short of becoming untethered. He grits his teeth to stall the pain. Silently, he pleads for the sound of police sirens and to hear their brakes screeching in answer to halting this whole fiasco. But nothing. Not a single siren is heard above the beating of the helicopter's rotor as it builds momentum in response to the engine's determined roar. Like a rag doll, Peter is tossed into the cockpit of an impatient bird waiting to take flight; landing in a tightly fitting seat behind the pilot. As the gun snags at his back, Peter is left as cold and rigid as marble. Hurriedly, the second Arab, who is tall and slim, leaps inside taking his seat in front of Kassri. Clicking shut their seatbelts, the pilot responds effortlessly to further instructions from Kassri, 'linadhhab,' let's go.

The engine bellows and the rotor whips encouraging the chopper to suck the ground before taking flight. A sharp tilt flings the cockpit eastward over London passing Big Ben, The Palace of Westminster and skirting The Houses of Parliament. As the tilt straightens, it makes its way down The River Thames to The Festival Hall and then sprints out towards The Tower of London. Periodically, as Peter presses his head against the window, the gun stabs at his ribs; a stark reminder of the perils he is having to endure. Pushing his forehead firmly against the window he tries to conceal the warm tears that fall down his flushed cheeks; not wishing for his gaolers to find a chink in his armour; clearly forgetting they'd already heard his squeals as early as when he opened the back door of his home. His vision is blurred from the vibrating window pressed on his forehead and tears that flood his ducts, but not sufficiently to blind his sight to see the helicopter's descent into London City Airport. Without moving his body, not wanting to alarm the shooter, Peter stretches his neck for a closer look. A rapid dialogue immediately begins inside his head, having found what he believes to be a chink in his captors' armour. *I don't have a passport. If there's one thing this country is good at, it's customs and security. The Home Office will have me returned to my sitting room in no time.*

The tall, thin Arab, sitting next to the pilot and who's been identified as Nader, passes the brown package to his partner in crime. Peter watches him stow it securely inside a pocket in his cream djellaba. *You might want to get your story straight about why you have that piece of art, sir,* thinks Peter. Guns are passed to the pilot who, whilst still continuing to steer the flight, reaches forward to wedge the weaponry beneath the controls. Kassri, sitting next to Peter, pulls out a leather clutch bag from under his seat and hands Peter a passport as he flashes an official looking document from *Drakes* The Auctioneers. *You have to be joking,* thinks Peter. *Your headed paper might fool someone but this passport will never wash,* until he opens the gold crested burgundy document and finds, what appears to be, an authentic looking passport.

The helicopter sucks the ground once more and hovers to find stability; righting itself before coming to rest. Two smartly uniformed VIP Customer Care Officers await to attend the chopper and guide its passengers safely away from the rotors that continue to spin as the engine ticks. A temporary shelter, nothing more than a prefabrication, is tasked with the formalities of passport and customs for private clients; where documents and luggage are duly checked.

Kassri tightens the grip on his prisoner's wrist. With every twist, Peter's skin screams, but all the while Mr Dowling considers his options; knowing this is probably his only chance. *No guns. No threat. It must be now,* he thinks.

'Excuse me officer,' calls Peter to the VIP care. 'I require public facilities prior to the flight. Could you direct me please?'

'Sir, your plane is ready to board where you will have all that you need.'

'No, you don't understand...' tries Peter again, only stalled by a sharp elbow burrowing into his left ribcage. 'Jesus...' shrieks Peter coughing and spluttering.

'Are you okay, sir?' asks the officer.

'No not really,' replies Peter, doubling down with excruciating pain.

'Please sir,' pleads the VIP officer to Peter, 'we are aware of the urgency for you to fly and are doing all we can to help.'

'Oh you are, are you?' replies Peter, struggling to catch his breath made worse by the full weight of Kassri standing on his big toe and slowly screwing it into the ground; purposefully and determinedly as if extinguishing a cigarette butt. The VIP officer crouches down to Peter's level and addresses him quietly and courteously.

Art For Art's Sake

'I am your VIP officer. I am fully briefed that you are very sick and a donor has been found for you. I promise we will have you to your destination with the utmost efficiency.'

A donor, thinks Peter, giving out a long moan as Kassri slowly starts to release his weight from Peter's toe where the pain increases ten fold, throbbing persistently inside his moccasin slipper.

'...errrrrr,' cries out Peter, causing his captors, without hesitation, to scoop him up. Nader and Kassri on either arm and Mr Dowling's feet once more, skimming the ground as he's whisked directly to the small private plane. The officer quickens his gait to ensure the comforts of his wealthy customers.

Kassri gives Peter a determined shove into a seat near the back of the plane beside the window; wedging him in by sitting next to him. The VIP customs officer stands at the front of the plane to ensure everything is as it should be and that his job is almost complete with another happy customer.

'Stop these people,' Peter shouts. 'I beg you,' he continues trying to stand up with his belt still buckled. 'These men are taking me against my will. They've kidnapped me from my London home. Please get help. Please get the police. You have to believe me.'

The blood drains from the officer leaving him as white as snow against his navy blue jacket.

'I tell you. Stop the plane, please,' continues Peter, refusing to sit down, even after receiving yet another thump from Kassri.

The VIP officer, unsure of what to do, is relieved by the interruption from Nader, who thanks him for his services. 'Shukran. Shukran,' says Nader, removing a small pile of £50 notes from a brown leather wallet and handing them to the officer. 'It's his medication. We are very sorry, please forgive him.'

'Oh thank you, sir. You are too kind.'

'Thank you for your help,' calls Kassri from the back of the plane continuing to hold and twist Peter's wrist; this time breaking the skin.

With nothing to lose at this juncture Peter calls out again to the VIP officer but on seeing him shaking hands with Nader, realises he's no match for the wad of £50 notes being tucked safely inside the officer's jacket. Instead, he watches his last hope leave the plane as instructions for take off, filter out from the cockpit.

'London City on the ground. Gulfstream Golf six fifer ze-ro. Requesting taxi for a SW departure with information November,' says, their pilot, Cedric Carlton-Smyth, in an utterly convincing Eastern European accent.

The plane taxis for take off. Peter's heart pounds. An image of the two women left inside his house flashes before him. *Did Nader shoot them both before closing his front door?*

'London City tower. Gulfstream Golf six fifer ze-ro Charlie November-Mike Sierra India Mike. Holding short,' relays Carlton-Smyth.

'Gulfstream Golf six fifer ze-ro cleared for take off,' informs Air Traffic Control.

'Gulfstream Golf six fifer ze-ro cleared for take off,' repeats Smyth.

Peter wriggles in his seatbelt and fumbles to unclip the buckle. Kassri, sitting close by, slaps him across the face but Peter can't be kept down. He finds strength from nowhere; helped by his confidence that London City have done their job and no guns are on board this plane. He pulls himself to his feet whilst his arms fling uncontrollably. 'How dare you do this to me,' he says. 'You can't do this to me. Stop the plane.'

'Hadi, hadi,' shouts Nader. Quiet, quiet.

'I want answers and I want them fast,' growls Peter in the lowest voice he can find.

'Sataerif fi ghdwn thlath saeat', says Kassri holding up three fingers in front of Mr Dowling's face. You will know in three hours time.

'I shall not wait three hours for information. Now. Tell me now.'

Nader tries to stand; pushing against the g-force as the plane gains momentum in preparation for take off. He manages to get closer to the back of the plane. Peter swivels his head in fast succession from Nader to Kassri and back again to Nader who is towering over him from the seat behind. Peter's heart beats faster. His eyes smart from the sweat running down his face. Nader reaches down to tug at Peter's arm and presses his shoulders tightly on the seat. Something cold and sharp scratches Peter's skin. He immediately feels limp; relaxed even. Then nothing.

CHAPTER THREE

Race against time

Anna-Belle Trait is quick to react; setting up an office in Peter's study with her mobile phone and tablet computer. She has already contacted the National Air Traffic Services (NATS) to request call signs and flight plans of all private jets that have taken off from London in the past thirty minutes and now she is focusing on the website, *Flights In Trace* that shows the movements of hundreds of flights in real time. Zooming in closer to the flights coming in and out of UK airspace she tries to make sense of the tiny planes that are constantly being recorded. Opening the attachment in the email from NATS, Anna-Belle is surprised by just how many private jets are in service, given the small percentage of the global population that can afford to own or hire such luxuries.

With the task she has in hand, Trait knows the importance of keeping Sarah onboard and turns the computer screen towards Henderson, who has not yet moved from behind the desk in the study or left the chair she was previously gagged and pinned.

Michelle Hockley

'Henderson, you are in for a real treat. We are about to play to your strengths.'

'I'm surprised you think I have any,' says Sarah.

'Well apparently you do, so listen up Henderson.'

'I'm listening.'

Trait shows Sarah the list of private jets that have left London in the last thirty minutes, along with their intended flight routes.

'Anyone of these flights,' Trait explains to Henderson, 'and subsequent flights sent to us from NATS as and when they leave London airspace, could be carrying Mr Dowling on board.'

'Well, that's assuming our fugitives are travelling private and not commercial,' replies Henderson, with her eyes fixed firmly on the data as she listens to her instructions.

'Sure, but we need to start somewhere, and it's more likely they went private,' says Trait, somewhat peeved that Henderson chooses a negative stance so early in proceedings.

'Okay, then private is the way we shall go. What do you want me to do?'

'Find the flight on which Mr Dowling and his captors are currently flying,' says Trait expecting at least a sigh or a gasp from Henderson but instead, completely unperturbed by the enormity of the task, Sarah, without hesitation, quickly starts to collate the facts available to her.

'So, given the attire and accent of the captors,' says Henderson, 'I am going to identify flights destined for North Africa and the Middle East. Would you agree?'

'Not necessarily Sherlock, but I hear what you are saying, and it's a start.'

'Okay,' begins Sarah, pointing to the area shown on the website, *Flights In Trace*, from Morocco to Syria. 'Our premise will be that they've taken a private plane to anywhere along these borders, including inland to say, Saudi Arabia or Sudan,' clearly relishing the prospect of getting her head down and diving into this task.

'Less talking Henderson and more cross checking,' replies Trait, clapping her hands to the rhythmic beat she expects Sarah to produce results; agitated by the prospect of stagnation that might deny any meaningful progress.

Trait reluctantly accepts the need to be patient and takes her leave in the kitchen with every intention of raiding Dowling's food cupboards. 'Bloody Hell,' says Anna-Belle with eyes wide as she opens Peter's fridge. 'The rich certainly know how to eat, I'll give em that. Pâté from where?' she asks, bringing the pot closer to her. 'Partridges? I thought only the likes of Posh and Becks shopped there. 'With her arms full of produce, her chin steadying the load, she closes the fridge door with her foot and lowers the contents onto the table.

Michelle Hockley

* * * * *

Monroe, still in his office at Blythe Street Police Station, sinks back into his chair trying to identify at which point this day went horribly wrong. The rest of his department, apart from those still out looking for two Arabs and Mr Dowling, are warming up to celebrate their colleague's birthday cheer.

'Knock knock sir,' shouts DC Cole as she enters Monroe's open office door and peers inside.

'Are you coming to join us? We're cutting the cake and you know how much you love a piece of sponge.'

'Sure, Cole, I'll be there. Have you done the speeches yet to remind DC Jacobs he's getting old?' asks Monroe.

'Sir, is anything wrong?' asks Cole. 'You look, well, done-in if you don't mind me saying?'

'No. I'm fine, nothing to see here. Move along Cole.'

'Okay, if you're sure. Victoria will make you feel better.'

'Who?'

'You know, Victoria Sponge.'

'Get out of here Cole and shut the door on your way out,' calls Monroe, throwing a paper clip at the now closed door.

Leaning back to reach his jacket pocket that's

draped over the back of his chair, he takes out a brand new SIM card. Opening the desk drawer, to choose one of the many pay-as-you-go phones, he unwraps the SIM and hurls the scrunched up cellophane towards the bin in the far corner of the room. Feeling isolated from the rest of the department on hearing a feint sound of celebration, *'Happy Birthday dear Big Feet. Should Be On The Beat. Happy Birthday to you. Hip Hip Hooray, Hip Hip Hooray, Hip Hip...'* he dials the telephone number from memory.

'This is the Voicemail service for 07710 501.. Please leave a message after the tone.'

'Carlton-Smyth. Where the Hell are you? You bastard.'

Monroe's heart beats with rage. He removes the SIM and returns the phone to the drawer; slamming it shut. 'You bastard. You bastard you.'

Opening his office door, the sound of the party rushes inside '...*for he's a jolly good fellow, for he's a jolly good fellow,*' and Monroe listens while slightly rooted to the floor.

'Monroe, at last,' says Cole, grabbing his arm. 'You've almost missed all the fun. We're about to give *Big Feet. Should Be On The Beat*, the bumps. Come on, have some cake, sir. Paper plates too, no single use plastic at this gathering.'

'Thank you Cole. Thank you.'

44

'Your welcome sir. Where's Henderson? Have you finally managed to shake her off, sir?'

'Don't know where she is. A law unto herself that one. And you'd do well to watch your tongue Cole, instead of bad mouthing colleagues.'

'Yes, sir. Apologies, sir.'

* * * * *

In Mr Dowling's kitchen, DS Anna-Belle Trait focusses on making a snack from the contents of his fridge.

'I hope you like pâté Henderson because that's what you've got,' shouts Anna-belle as she waits for the toaster to pop up.

'Trait,' shouts Sarah from the study. 'Listen, I'm starting to get something relevant.'

'What is it Henderson? I'm all ears. Shoot,' leaping into the study to take a closer look.

The computer screen on the tablet shows hundreds of tiny aeroplanes, and even smaller ones for private jets, looking not too dissimilar to Flying Ant Day. Anna-Belle Trait circles her hand to encourage Henderson to get to the point, much much quicker.

'Okay,' starts Henderson. 'These are the private jets that have taken off from either Heathrow, Farnborough, Biggin Hill, Gatwick and London City and destined for the part of the world we are interested in.'

'What? No. All of these? We are in double figures. I thought we were getting somewhere,' drawing her finger down the list of call sign numbers that Henderson has highlighted.

'Yep, I'm afraid so. It's a large area that we are covering. You have to admit though, it's considerably narrowed down from the hundreds of flights currently in the air as we speak.'

'Well yes, but the private planes you've listed could all be loss leaders. We are wasting time and the longer this goes on we are losing Mr Dowling.'

'Can we contact each of these pilots?' asks Sarah.

'Well supposing one of them was our target. Once they knew we were on to them, they'd instantly either change course or go further undercover. We'd definitely lose Dowling then. Forever.'

'They might not even be in a private plane or even going to the area I've suggested,' says Sarah somewhat deflated by the number of obstacles.

'Exactly. There are just too many ifs and buts. For all we know, Dowling could be flying in a hot air balloon.'

'Wait, I've got an idea,' exclaims Henderson changing the current web page to another setting. 'Give me two minutes,' already buckling down to further research, without waiting for an answer from her superior in rank.

'Henderson stop,' shouts Trait, conscious of the minutes that have already been fruitless, knowing every second lost, puts Dowling in greater danger.

'Shush. Shush,' replies Sarah, flicking her hand to indicate she needs Anna-belle to go away for just a few more minutes.

'Okay, but only two minutes,' says Anna-Belle, backing away towards the kitchen, feeling slightly ill-at-ease in a moment of subservience. She picks up her half eaten sandwich and pulls herself up to sit and perch on the kitchen counter; wincing as she hears Monroe's voice in her head berating her for not being on her mark at the market to collect Dowling's package. *Monroe's right. I'm responsible for this mess. Which means I'm responsible for what is happening to Dowling right now. Damn you Monroe.* Jumping down from the kitchen counter, brushing away crumbs from her jeans, she takes a plate of food to Sarah.

'Come on Henderson, time's up. Come on. Let's go,' says Anna-Belle, placing the pâté down in front of Henderson.

'I think I've got something,' replies Sarah.

'Halle *blooming* lujah,' replies Anna-Belle as she kneels down beside the desk taking a closer look at the screen that Henderson has been pouring over.

'Okay. Are you listening?' says Sarah.

'Yes, more than you can possibly imagine,' says Anna-Belle, getting comfortable.

'Okay, whatever,' replies Sarah, taking a quick glance at Trait, who she is sure is a little strange.

'Come on Henderson, speak faster. Please, I'm begging you.'

'Okay. I've found three private jets that came into the UK this morning, from either North Africa or the Middle East and have also departed from London within our time frame.'

'Three possibilities, that's good, but not wanting to burst your bubble, Henderson, we don't know our plane arrived in the UK this morning,' says Trait.

'It's all supposition at this stage; a viable hypothesis.'

'Okay. If this hypothesis is viable, how will this particular scenario play-out then?' replies Trait as Sarah scuffles to find a clean page in her notebook to draw a diagram to explain more carefully.

'So, this plane's tail number, CN-MISM. A Gulfstream 650, which, may I add, is a beautiful plane.'

'Don't mess with me Henderson, I don't care about the quality of the plane.'

'Well, for the record, it's a pretty good plane. Anyway, it departed from Marrakesh Menara Airport. Menara means minaret, perhaps in reference to the calling towers of a mosque,' Sarah adds, feeling that her thought process requires some added context.

'Again Henderson. Still not interested.'

'It's history. You should be interested.'

'And it's the past. Gone. Finished. Over. Kaput.'

'Well, I could argue that opinion away in a matter of seconds, given that history is cyclical.'

'Well, fortunately, we don't have surplus time, so can we continue with trying to rescue Mr Dowling who is very much of the present, if you don't mind?'

'Sure. This particular plane, CN-MISM, departed Marrakesh at 9am local time, and arrived today, London City Airport at 11.40 UK time. Then departs the UK at 15.00 which means if it returns to Marrakesh, where it is routed, it will arrive at 19.40 local time. If that's our plane, we have our target.

'Okay, but it's still very light weight and flimsy. What else do you have?'

'I've done exactly the same for the other two flights that came in today; one from Cairo and the other from Riyadh. Both landed within a two hour window of each other, all before 14.00, which was the time Mr Dowling's captors arrived at the house. One of these came into Gatwick and the other, Biggin Hill.'

'Its a start Henderson, but that is all it is. There are still too many uncertainties.'

Sarah puts down her pen, her eyes blinking as she leans back in her chair, knowing she has some distance to go with this conundrum. 'This really is a needle in a haystack,' says Sarah. 'All we are doing is imposing what could be fact on something that might be possible.'

'A priori,' says Trait, grinning, for having used a word that might surprise the boffin that sits before her.

'Not exactly. We do have empirical evidence, but quite honestly, we don't have enough.'

'No, we sure don't,' says Trait, starting to pace the floor.

'Shall I let Monroe know we've drawn a blank?' asks Henderson.

'I'll call Monroe,' replies Trait, 'maybe this is one for Interpol,' she adds, leaving the study for the sitting room to make a call back to base.

Sarah catches sight of the tray of food that Anna-Belle brought in earlier and being careful not to drop chutney on the thick plush pile beneath her feet, starts to drizzle chutney over the pâté that is supported by an overly large slice of wholemeal bread. Yet, her enjoyment of such luxurious produce is somewhat marred by the fact she's been unable to find a solution to their problem and instead of eating, she stares at Google's empty search bar that is begging to be challenged.

'Okay Google, try this for size,' typing, private jet + service + Gatwick. Enter. The results certainly provide some possible links, causing Sarah to sit up and take a closer look at Google's suggestions. Clicking on the first link, after the advert, she brings up a very highly polished website that displays a rather smiley chap

50

looking back at her, who apparently, is here to help ones every need.

'In your dreams, sunshine. You are getting nowhere near my every needs, not unless you have a telephone number to your VIP establishment,' says Sarah, picking up her pâté lunch, taking a bite as she scrolls the site in search of a phone number. *Why did society give up so readily on the act of talking on the telephone in favour of emails?*

'Gotcha' 01293 4633... Thank you. Now Google, try doing the same for Biggin Hill and London City.'

In the adjacent room, Anna-Belle is bringing Monroe up to speed.

'This whole episode stinks,' says Monroe.

'It does a bit sir,' replies Trait.

'I mean, who the hell knew that piece of art even existed, apart from, Dowling, the client, you, me, and Carlton-Smyth?'

'Goodness knows. Have you spoken to Carlton-Smyth?' asks Trait. 'What does he advise?'

'He doesn't answer his phone. He's a slime ball that one. He'd be happy to leave us in the do dos.'

'According to Dowling, Carlton-Smyth's in the Serengeti. Have you heard that?' asks Trait.

'Serengeti? Don't make me laugh. If he's more than a mile from a five star hotel with whirl pool, he'd be hyperventilating.'

'I've got to go, I can hear Henderson calling and with any luck she might be closer to locating Dowling, even if we've said good bye to the artwork,' says Trait, closing down her call and making her way quickly to the study.

'Okay, Henderson, I'm all ears,' jumping onto the desk in the study, and crossing her legs, causing Sarah to jump back.

'Can't you just be normal Trait? Now listen. For the three flights we are interested, I've contacted the VIP officers, or whatever they call themselves, those that promise to look after the smooth running of passengers who arrive at airports using a private plane.'

'Yes, yes,' replies Trait, once more wishing Sarah could learn that every second counts.

'I've contacted each of their security departments and am waiting to receive CCTV footage of the passengers on these flights, as they came in and left the UK.'

'Good work Henderson. Good job.'

'I've managed to speak to the VIP officer at London City. He's been really helpful confirming that this plane,' pointing to the call sign on the list, 'carried a passenger who was leaving the country at speed after finding a match.'

'A match? What's that?'

'You know, organ donor. A match?'

'Oh. Well we can rule that one out then.'

'Yes, I agree. I shall let you know when the CCTV footage arrives or I get to speak to the VIP officers at Gatwick and Biggin Hill.'

'At last, we might be cooking,' says Trait, swinging herself down from the desk to fire off a text to arrange for fingerprints to be taken in Dowling's house; something that should have been done straight away. *Monroe is definitely losing his touch,* she thinks.

'Eureka...! shouts Sarah.

'Have we got something?' says Trait.

'You bet we have. 'Look at this image from London City Airport.'

'But I thought the passenger at London City....'

'Look Trait, it's Mr Dowling. He's got his slippers on. He won't like that.'

'Is this another plane? I thought the VIP at London City said the passenger was a patient,' says Trait.

'It's the same plane. It's the one travelling to Marrakesh at speed because they'd found a match. I didn't cancel the CCTV and now I'm so glad I didn't. That was obviously their Modus Operandi.'

'We need to go now,' says Anna-Belle closing down the computer and collecting her belongings, whilst muttering to Henderson, that if she wants to survive at Blythe Street nick, she needs to drop the Latin.

'Where are we going?' calls out Sarah, running to

collect her things together, being swept up with Trait's excitement.

'Marrakesh, that's where. The Menara.'

'Shouldn't we...I don't know....shouldn't we,' stutters Sarah, not cut out for spur of the moment travel or anything that hasn't been planned with an inch of its life.

'Shut it Henderson,' says Trait as she dials to speak to Monroe. 'It's Trait. We've located Dowling.'

'Bravo. Well done. Any sign of that snake Carlton-Smyth?'

'No nothing on him yet, but then we've not been looking for him have we.'

'Where's Dowling?' asks Monroe.

'He's heading in a private jet to Marrakesh. We are going to bring him back. Can you phone ahead to the Menara airport and request they hold him and his abductors until we get there. They land at 19.40 hours local time. '

'Not so fast DS Trait,' calls back Monroe. 'This case is now for Interpol or National Crime Agency abroad. We can't step on their toes.'

'We can if you give me permission. Come on Monroe, we know the form. If we get them involved, we shall have to answer so many questions. Come on. What do you say?'

'Yes, you are probably right. Go on then.'

'Yes, sir,' shouts Trait.

'Give me the details then,' says Monroe sounding more than apprehensive.

'Are you ready?' says Trait.

'Yes, ready,' replies Monroe.

'Registration Charlie November-Mike India Sierra Mike a Gulfstream 650...'

'...Cor!' interrupts Monroe. 'A Gulfstream 650? Very nice too.'

'Don't you start Monroe, I've had all that from Henderson. What's wrong with you all?'

'Okay, got it. Off you go.'

'Thank you sir,' replies Trait. 'Come on Henderson we've got the go ahead. I trust you have your passport?'

'Of course I do. What did you mean about finding someone else? Who else is missing? Who else are we looking for?'

'Not now Henderson. Let's find Dowling and do our bit by the innocent. We'll take the Harley.'

'You are joking.'

'I'm not,' calls out Trait, throwing a spare helmet up to Sarah, still on the top step after slamming shut Peter Dowling's front door.

'There is nothing normal about you whatsoever, Trait. I don't care if you are my senior. You are not normal.'

Art For Art's Sake

Obeying orders, Henderson buckles the strap beneath her chin; adjusting herself on the pillion to find a position that will reduce her chances of dying. Anna-Belle, so relieved to be back in control opens the throttle and turns over the engine a couple of times. Sarah, on the other hand, sits back with a firm grip and rues the moment she decided to combine her late lunch with a visit to Dowling's house to update him on the missing person.

CHAPTER FOUR

Touch Down

Trait and Henderson near the end of their flight. 'Ladies and Gentlemen, this is your captain speaking. We shall shortly be landing at Menara airport making our arrival time of twenty two hundred hours. We have been requested, by local police, to remain seated whilst they board the plane to carry out routine checks. I am assured, this will not delay any connecting flights. On behalf of *Jupiter Airlines*, I thank you for your co-operation and wish you a pleasant stay or onward journey.'

Passengers start to shift in their seats; unnerved by the need for police to board the plane. Sarah nudges Trait for her reaction to *routine checks;* a term both unconvincing and always loaded. Trait doesn't respond. Staying perfectly still, holding a poker face, her eyeline skimming the headrest of the seat in front. Sarah is embarrassed that two members of the Metropolitan Police are as oblivious to what is happening and slides a little down her seat, praying that nothing is on display that can identify their profession.

Michelle Hockley

The plane makes its final decent causing Sarah's ears to fill up and her stomach to flip. If this was a vacation, she'd be lapping up the prospect of an adventure at this point, eager to discover new and interesting facts about her destination. Yet coming here in a work capacity, and knowing nothing about Moroccan law she feels very much out of her depth. She knows it's a straightforward act, to bring Dowling back to the UK, but hopes to God, that Trait has a smattering of North Africa's legal procedure to know what to do when the abductors start to explain themselves. Reassuring herself that Monroe will have brought the UK International Crime Bureau and the Anti Kidnap and Extortion Unit of the National Crime Agency up to speed by now, she relaxes and concentrates on the landing.

Glistening beneath the airport lights are two 4x4's marked, *Surété, Nationale.* Uniformed officers wait beside their vehicles as the plane comes to a stand still. Inside the plane it is silent, except for one passenger who is quick to unleash the seatbelt and reach into the overhead locker to retrieve his bag. Sarah's eyes are glued to the *runaway passenger.* She's ready to make a leap and bring him down. The air-hostess quietly reminds the eager passenger to remain seated, which he does without confrontation; apologetic of his actions, which Sarah suspects, are a default setting to the end of every plane journey. Doors soon open at the front of the aeroplane and two police officers walk towards the rear of the plane; stopping as they come to seat 23a and 23b, where Sarah takes a sharp intake of breath.

'Miss Trait?' asks the policeman. 'Can I see your passport.'

Anna-Belle turns towards Sarah with a furrowed brow, clearly puzzled and hands over her passport.

'You, Miss Trait, are under arrest. Please, your hands,' requests the officer, slinging on handcuffs that are handed to him from the officer standing closely behind.

Sarah's heart already hyper, increases its race twofold as she comes eye to eye with the officer's impassive expression. Waiting for the cuffs to be slung her way, she doesn't dare move a muscle, instead keeping a straight face, giving nothing. The officer turns away from Sarah and unbuckles Trait's seatbelt and yanks her to standing. The overhead locker is pulled down sharply, and Trait is asked to identify her luggage before being escorted down the plane with one police officer in front and one behind.

Inside the terminal building Sarah can't get to her phone quick enough to call Monroe, but after three rings – she is met with a voice mail asking to leave a message. 'Damn,' says Sarah through gritted teeth, 'his phone should be on at all times.'

Scrolling down her contacts, her hands noticeably

shaking, she finds DS Cole whose desk is not far from Monroe's office.

'Cole,' shouts Sarah.

'Who is this?' Cole replies.

'Who do you think, Cole? Look on the screen before answering.'

'Oh. It's you Henderson. The wanderer returns. Where have you been all day? No one knows where you are, ever,' Cole replies, with the emphasis on *ever,* which Sarah chooses to ignore.

'Is Monroe there, Cole?'

'He's not here. He left about two hours ago.'

'Where's he gone?'

'He didn't say. Though he was looking a little peaky which wasn't down to the Victoria sponge because I made that and it was fresh.'

'What? Oh never mind, don't answer that Cole. Can you go into his office and see if he's left his mobile on his desk please?'

'Yes, but it's late you know,' says Cole pausing briefly at the office door, a little surprised it's closed shut. On entering she scans the room. 'No, the desk is clear, Henderson. No phone on the desk.'

'Can you check his drawer before I make the assumption he's in a tunnel or down a cellar somewhere.'

Cole opens the desk drawer. 'Good grief.'

'What is it Cole? Talk to me.'

'Oh my dear God.'

'What is it?' repeats Sarah Henderson.

'There's a whole drawer of phones.'

'Can you dial his number from the land-line and see if they ring.'

Cole does as she's asked and makes the call, standing over the open drawer that's crammed full of phones.

'Nothing Henderson. None of these phones are his number,' she says, starting to open and shut all the drawers in the desk.

'Cole,' shouts Henderson. 'Are you still there? Cole, talk to me.'

'Yes, still here,' she replies slowly, somewhat distracted as she pulls out from one of the drawers, an envelope attached to a smart phone, addressed to DS Trait.

'What is going on Cole? You've gone very quiet,' says Henderson.

'There's a letter addressed to Trait in Monroe's handwriting,' says Cole holding it up in front of herself. 'Were they having a thing?'

'I've no idea. Isn't that type of information gathering more your area of expertise?'

Cole sniggers to herself; fully aware that Henderson has a low opinion of the team at Blythe Street with them not being her cup of tea.

Michelle Hockley

'Can you switch the phone on, Cole? If there's life in it, dial Monroe's number from the land line to confirm if this is his phone.'

'Yep, this is his phone. He's left his mobile phone. It's wiped clear of contacts too. Why would he do that? Oh no. His badge is here,' says Cole holding it up to the desk lamp.

'Okay Cole. You may as well know. I'm at the airport in Marrakesh. I'm here to bring an abductee back to the UK.'

'How did all that happen?'

'It's a long story. But the short version is, that DS Trait has been arrested.'

'Crikey, you have been busy.'

'Well don't just stand there, go and let the Chief Superintendent know what is going on.'

'I'm on to it, Henderson,' replies Cole, picking up the things left behind by Monroe. 'Do you want me to read the letter to you?' asks Cole.

'No. Just take everything to the Chief Super.'

Sarah ends the call and scans her surroundings in the airport, noticing just how shattered she is feeling. Seeing a door marked *Airport Police* brings immediate solace and she feels a surge of energy giving her a second wind as she knocks for attention. A broad shouldered woman in a uniform, that is clearly too small for her, opens the door and holds a gaze that emanates a strong, don't mess with me, attitude.

'Good evening,' says Sarah Henderson. 'I am from the Metropolitan Police in London,' fumbling for her badge and displaying it proudly. 'I understand you are retaining passengers from a recent arrival on orders from a DCI Monroe. The plane arrived today at 19.40 hours from London City, in the UK.'

The officer looks confused and stares blankly. Sarah holds up her badge again, 'Metropolitan. London,' she says. The officer steps aside inviting Sarah to enter the office and take a seat. The room is small and musty; furnished with the bare minimum of what might be required. The scratched wooden desk is barely visible for being weighed down by an overbearing computer monitor whose back bulges beyond the edge of the table spewing multiple cables that cascade down to the brown threaded carpet. A ceiling fan rotates furiously, but for its efforts produces very little in the way of a breeze. Sarah occupies the low-slung, off white, leather chair and in what seems like slow-motion, watches the officer side step her way behind the desk that is positioned tight against the wall; taking great care to avoid knocking off the overhanging clunky keyboard in order to render more room so she can take her seat.

'Now,' says the officer ready to assist. 'You say, Metropolitan Police, London.'

'Yes. Can you tell me please where you are

holding the passengers from the aircraft, CN-MISM please?'

At the touch of the keyboard, the computer wakes from *sleep mode,* straining itself, appearing exhausted before it has begun.'

'Let us take a look for you, madam.'

Sarah feels herself becoming irritated by the lack of urgency shown her. After all, she thinks, *I'm here on official business for the Met. I'm not reporting a lost baggage.* Though she appreciates just how distressing that too can be, having been separated from her luggage for most of her last holiday.

'Don't worry yourself,' snaps Sarah, I shall contact Interpol. This should have been with them anyway,' recalling how Anna-Belle was determined to stop Monroe from getting anyone else involved; begging him almost to allow her to go and rescue Mr Dowling herself.

'I have the database here,' says the officer. 'The call-sign, CM, you say,' entering the letters.

'No. It's CN, Charlie, November. The plane is registered in Morocco. CN,' replies Sarah, raising her voice, displaying obvious signs of being unable to hold her frustration for a moment longer. A show of discontent that is doing nothing to hurry proceedings but instead highlighting just how ill prepared she is for such an intervention on foreign soil.

'Yes, here it is,' says the officer. 'Arrival today, at

19.40 hours. A private jet. Gulfstream 650.'

'Yes, thank you. Can you take me to the passengers please?'

'No. We are not holding any passengers from that time. Should they have been?'

'Indeed yes. Our request was made this afternoon, for the passengers to be retained.'

'No. Nothing here. I'm sorry. We have not received such a request.'

'Are you sure? Please would you mind checking again?'

'I can be sure we have no instructions of that nature,' says the officer with eyes firmly fixed on the computer screen, clearly not wishing to make a mistake.

Sarah tries to think on her feet. If nothing else, she must at least make some enquiries to track down Mr Dowling. She asks for details of the plane's registered owner, which, if she'd had time, would have found before leaving London.

'Oh yes, I can give you that information. Registered to J. Kassri, at an address in Rabat.'

'Erm... Kassri?' repeats Sarah mulling over the name she hears.

'Yes, that's right, J. Kassri. Registered in Rabat,' confirms the officer, with eyes still fixed to the screen, as she double and triple checks the information she is giving before writing down the registered address to give to Henderson.

'Thank you,' says Sarah, tucking the piece of paper into her handbag and getting out her boarding pass to show the officer. 'Can you direct me to DS Trait who was removed from this flight, please.'

'One moment please,' says the officer, clicking to another page on the computer.

Sarah feels her knee begin to bounce and her heel jerk up and down; a habit she revisits to focus her concentration and silence her anxiety. Clinging to her phone, that rests on a somewhat uneven lap with the bouncing, she looks down in anticipation of a call from the Chief Superintendent to guide her through this maze before she messes up and is forced to join Trait. The officer hands Sarah her boarding pass having noted the relevant details. 'Thank you,' says, Sarah using it immediately to fan her face.

'I see here,' starts the officer relaying information from her screen. 'A request was raised at 20.00 hours from Detective Chief Inspector, Monroe, of Metropolitan Police, for the arrest of Miss Anna-Belle Trait.'

A request from Monroe? Thinks Sarah. *That can't be right. What is Monroe playing at? He leaves his badge, calls for Trait's arrest. No. There has to be some mistake.*

'Where is she now? I need to see her?'

'*Sûreté Nationale*, Avenue Houmman el Fetouaki, Marrakesh, 40000,' adds the officer, taking out a glossy map from her drawer and circling the relevant address and telephone number with her Biro pen.

'You don't understand. They've arrested the wrong person,' says Sarah, as she takes the map being handed to her; a document she feels falls far short of the gravitas of the current situation.

'I have no more information, marm. You need to go to *Sûreté Natio...*'

'...thank you,' interjects Sarah. 'Can I trouble you to recommend a riad at this late hour please?' she says, handing back the folded map for another gush of Biro.

'This one is very good, not far from Badi Palace and you can take a taxi direct to the door.'

'Sorry, direct to the door? As opposed to what?' enquires Sarah, immediately embarrassed by how tetchy she has become again.

'A taxi cannot drive into the Medina, the streets are too narrow. You have to walk and now it's late you might not find your way.'

Too right, thinks Sarah. 'Thank you, you've been most helpful.'

'Afwan,' replies the officer, standing up to escort Sarah through to Passport Control and Customs.

Outside of the airport, it is warm and clammy. The rich, exotic smells that Sarah expected of Marrakesh, immediately come to life. She telephones the *Sûreté Nationale,* but after making it quite clear several times, in different tones ranging from friendly to authoritative that she is DC Henderson from the Metropolitan Police, she is nonetheless, given short shrift and asked to call back in the morning. Standing somewhere about the taxi rank, but not totally committed to the queue, the taxi driver shouts from the car window.

'Madame, you want taxi?'

'Oh, erm. Yes. Rue de Berrima, please,' showing the circle on the map through the window to compensate for her poor pronunciation.

'Yes, near El Badi.'

'Shukran,' replies Sarah, entering the back of the taxi just as her phone starts to ring.

'Chief Superintendent. Thank you for coming back to me.'

'DC Henderson you are doing a great job. We are getting up to speed here in London and advise that you take a morning flight back to the UK.'

'Yes, Chief, but what about DS Trait, sir. There's been a terrible mistake. She's been falsely arrested. Should I at least try to get a meeting with her? Do you have all the facts sir? What of Mr Dowling?'

'I appreciate your concerns Henderson and we thank you. However, your orders are to make your way back to Blythe Street tomorrow morning. We shall deal with everything else.'

'But sir, what about...I mean, don't you need to

know more details. All the details?'

'Henderson. It's late. Get some sleep and return in the morning.'

'Yes, sir, I shall,' she replies, backing off, acutely aware of where she comes in the hierarchy. She puts the phone into her handbag as a way of signing off for the day and uses the journey from the airport to the outskirts of the Median, to contemplate the sequence of events that has led to her being the last man standing.

CHAPTER FIVE

In Deep

The Riad Karma is a heavenly sanctuary; granting DC Sarah Henderson the luxury of a sound night's sleep. Without further word from the Chief Superintendent, she accepts the orders given her last night and affords occupancy to the environs that lie before her. Breakfast is served on the roof terrace beneath the flawless blue sky and a gentle heat emerges to greet a new day. The spiced aromas captivate her senses and her gaze, for a moment, is transfixed on the beauty of the Ciconiidae storks, whose nests occupy each of the turrets in the ruins of the Badi Palace.

'Good Morning, madam,' says the general manager. 'I trust everything has been to your satisfaction.'

'Indeed yes. Very much so, thank you.'

'A car is arriving to take you to the airport in one hour. I hope you will find the time to savour what our city has to offer.'

'I shall certainly do my best in the time I have,' replies Sarah, armed with her glossy map for directions to take her to the famous, Jemaa el-Fnaa square.

Outside the hotel, the ambience is incomparable to the sanctuary that was held within the courtyard of the Riad Karma. The narrow street is a popular route where high energy persists among the crowds going towards their daily chores and employment. Mopeds weave in and out of the crowds and rev impatiently behind Sarah's heels to gain unfettered access and be on their way.

'Come inside my friend,' calls one shopkeeper, followed by another and another in quick succession; hoping to entice a sale with the allure of the leather slippers that display themselves in every vibrant colour imaginable. Sarah manages to resist, not only because she's afraid of missing her flight, but also not wanting to cause mayhem by crossing someone's path to take a look.

But even with Sarah keeping in line, there is no abating to the commotion and as the lane narrows further ahead, the chaos increases. Shoulders bump against each other and mopeds prevail with intent. She wonders if in fact it's worth carrying on. *I mean,* she thinks, *just how spectacular does a square need to be to tolerate such disorder.* She takes a quick glance at her watch as she apologises for the umpteenth time for others encroaching on her personal space. But this time, it's different. She's almost knocked sideways. Her arm is grabbed with forced pressure and a rough assault persists; pushing her along in the direction she was intending to travel. With her arm twisted back on itself, far up into her scapular, she's left with insufficient mobility to take sight of her attacker. Crowds close in on her as they continue to inch past and hot breath expels into her ear from the whisper of a British, male, public school accent.

'Keep walking. Look straight ahead and no one will get hurt.'

Sarah tenses her whole body. Her elbow, seemingly being used as a rudder on a boat, steers her through the crowds beyond the square and into a maze of tiny streets. She tries again to glimpse her assailant by defying the pressure on her neck, but the struggle against her increases and she is forced back to a neutral gaze.

'You won't get away with this,' rumbles Sarah without moving her lips for fear of drawing attention to herself and harbouring unwanted aggression.

Against her will, Sarah's feet rattle through the narrow lanes that are now scarcely the width of two people. Vendors are busy selling their wares with barely a whisker between them. Scrunching herself smaller whilst still in an enforced arm-lock, she manages to squeeze past the units, avoiding the open shutters as sellers slap raw meat for sale onto their front counters. Blood splatters from the carcasses causing cats to jump up and join in the fayre. The hold on her arm digs ever deeper; nails pierce through her skin. A wooden hand cart, making deliveries, drives straight towards them with no intention of stopping or swerving. With seconds to spare, before a head on collision, her attacker finally frees her arm from his grasp, causing a centrifugal force to come up fast. She hits against the side of a shed bouncing off and landing on fruit and vegetables laid on the ground for sale along the lane.

Shaken and confused, Sarah starts to move her limbs beneath the dregs of wilting leaves and black bananas.

'Inshallah. Inshallah.' *If Allah wills it,* says the woman who remains seated alongside the stall that Sarah has just destroyed.

I don't think this is God's will, thinks Sarah, as she gets to her feet, looking around for her aggressor who she sees is trying to free himself from the wheel of the wooden cart.

'I know you,' bellows Sarah, stumbling to gain her balance. 'You're Cedric Carlton-Smyth. You better have a good reason for your behaviour because I'm Met police,' she says, continuing to catch her feet in tarpaulin that guards against damage to the already over ripened produce.

'Malcolm said you'd taken the role of DC,' shouts Carlton-Smyth from the wheel in which he has become embedded.

'Who the hell is Malcolm?' answers Sarah, reaching for her wallet to pay the poor woman for the trouble she's been caused.

'Shukran. Shukran,' replies the woman, who although somewhat shaken, smiles as Sarah holds both her hands and apologises before bidding her farewell.

'Okay, Carlton-Smyth I have a flight to catch so I shall leave you to your James Bond, 007 antics. A car is waiting to take me to the airport,' says Sarah.

'You won't be making that flight, nor any flight,' starts Smyth grabbing her arm once more, having been freed from the wheel.

'Get off me,' she replies, tugging her arm back and rubbing her shoulder. 'You've done enough damage in the past few minutes.'

'You have to come with me, they know you have evidence.'

'What are you talking about you silly man. Who? Where? How did you even know I was in Marrakesh?'

'Malcolm.'

'Again. Who is Malcolm?'

'DCI Monroe,' replies Smyth leaving Sarah struck as she tries to process that piece of information. *How does Monroe have anything to do with Smyth?* she thinks. *If nothing else, they are socially worlds apart to the absolute extreme. Unless,* she thinks, *it's the Freemasons,* knowing such a fraternity still exists.

Crowds start once more to busy themselves; returning to their transactions, quickly resuming to a level of normality after the unexpected interlude to accommodate the crash between them and the cart. Voices start to chatter. Wooden trolleys pass with the same undue care and mopeds buzz as they gather speed. Sarah is intrigued by Carlton-Smyth's presence and fumbles for her notebook. With barely enough room to reach inside her handbag she scrambles for a pen.

'Bingo,' she says, on finally locating all of her equipment; brushing away strands of hair from her eyes that have stuck fast from the heat of the day.

'Right, Mr Carlton-Smyth, what can you tell me about....' says Sarah, unable to complete her sentence on catching sight of two Moroccan men; one stout and one tall walking closer towards her.

Smyth, facing in the opposite direction to Sarah, focuses on Sarah's vagueness. 'Tell you about what...? What?' says Smyth.

A flashback to Dowling's house confirms her instant fear of the men she sees in the distance; feeling the cord tight around her mouth and hearing a gunshot before the door slammed shut on Dowling's house. Her first thoughts are to run. Go back to the riad and take the car that waits to drive her to the airport. *I can't do that,* she thinks. *The very reason for being in Marrakesh is to have these men brought to justice and return Dowling to the UK. How would I explain that to the Chief; coming face to face with Mr Dowling's assailants and then running away without asking questions? No. I need to stand my ground.* The men gain on her, getting closer. She tries to remember which pocket she might find her badge so that she can grab it quickly and appear professional. She stares firmly in their direction. *These are mine for the taking and by all accounts, a worthy mention in dispatches*, she thinks. Flexing her muscles; remaining solid in her foundation, she reminds herself that she still knows nothing about Moroccan law and will need to blag it. The pair move closer towards her. Her eyes remain fixed on the prize. Within a tacit beat, the two Arabs, one on either side, sweep her up and deposit her inside a waiting Calèche. With no time to gather her thoughts, the horse drawn carriage bounces on its springs, throwing her sideways where she skims the pink tasselled canopy before landing squashed between the two Arabs on the padded bench seat. Smyth stands at the archway to the Medina watching the carriage fade into the distance.

'Who are you?' shouts Sarah still bouncing about, trying to right herself, pulling herself from their grip. 'What do you want? I am Metropolitan Police.'

Kassri at last speaks, 'you know Mr Dowling?'

'Yes. What have you done with him? Where is he?' she shouts.

'You know Carlton-Smyth.'

'Yes. So what if I do? What is this all about?' realising she's putting aside the fact that these men have no qualms about using a shooter.

The carriage turns onto the main highway and joins alongside the everyday traffic of cars and trucks. Speed increases as the whip slashes pinning Sarah into her seat. The noise of traffic increases as the horse rushes forth. No longer able to hear or be heard she starts instead to take a mental note of any landmarks should she get the opportunity to call for help.

Twenty minutes into their journey, heading north east, the Calèche slows almost to a halt on entering *Palmeraie*, where buildings, in stark contrast to those of the Medina, take on the guise of a highly polished Hollywood movie set. Palatial homes, uniquely fashioned for the dignified rich, are framed to perfection by gardens designed with military precision.

'Huna. Huna. Aneataf yamina,' shouts Nader. Here, turn right.

The carriage turns into an elongated drive that stretches far into the distance of their destination; flanked by the tallest and straightest palm trees of equal proportions. At the end of the driveway, beside the front door, the carriage comes to a stand still.

Inside the house, Sarah is instructed to wait in the vestibule beneath an arch of white lace stucco carving and decoration of mosaic tiles of pink and cream. A woman enters carrying a silver teapot on a silver tray, dressed in a beautifully pressed grey djellaba with a white embroidered collar. Sarah watches the woman take the utmost pride in her duty; pouring a wide arc of hot fresh mint tea into a small glass. Sarah is at once confused and very suspicious. One minute these men are rough, stopping at nothing, and now they are offering tea in the most tranquil of settings. *Perhaps hospitality is key,* she thinks. *Maybe if Mr Dowling had been more hospitable to these people in his home, we wouldn't be in this mess.*

'Shukran,' says Sarah taking the glass encased in the shiniest of silver.

'Afwan,' replies the woman quietly as she steps back a few paces to stand against the wall.

Sarah inhales the mint vapour coming off the tea wondering if it's safe to drink. *It could be drugged,* she thinks and so remains perfectly still, not caring to move from the polished marble floor that brings additional coolness to proceedings. The maid holds out the teapot and nods her head which Sarah assumes is to encourage her to go ahead and drink. *Mrs Maid,* thinks Sarah smiling and raising her glass, *you don't know, like I do, just how brutal your employers are. They will stop at nothing. Put a foot wrong Missy and you could find yourself this afternoon being sold to join a caravan of camels or worse.* Sarah stops her babbling on seeing now as an opportunity to contact the Chief Super and tell him she's located the assailants or rather they've located her. Putting down her glass on the floor she gets out her phone.

'Ah. No. No,' says the maid stepping away from the wall, still holding her tray with one hand, tutting and wagging her index finger at Sarah with the other.

'I'm sorry, of course, your beautiful floor. I didn't think,' says Sarah picking up the glass and handing it to the maid as she continues to scroll for the Chief Superintendent's number.

'Ah. No. No,' repeats the maid, holding her hand to her ear.

'It's a personal call,' says Sarah, over pronouncing her words eager not to be misunderstood. 'Friends and family,' as she holds her phone aloft, waving it from side to side; catching site of a number of missed calls and wishing one of them at least, might be DS Trait coming to find her.

Without hesitation, the maid picks up a heavy brass, ornate, hand-bell that stands on the small table nearby. Sarah leaps back into place and slips the phone back into her bag; not knowing if the maid is going to call for help to control this unruly visitor that stands before her, or lob it over the visitor's head. Either way, the maid seems to be briefed on more than just the gentle act of eloquently pouring tea. Sarah shows her that the phone has been put away, hoping to placate the unpleasant atmosphere that this false move has brought about and return swiftly to something more cordial.

Like a clap of thunder, a woman's cry calls out in horrific pain from another room. The echo bounces off the marble floor creating an excruciating hollow noise. Sarah flinches on hearing a woman's tormented grief. *Jesus, is this a house of torture? Am I standing here waiting to be tortured?* The maid doesn't react. Her eyes remain fixed. The tray of tea is perfectly balanced. The screaming subsides but Sarah's heart quickens. A door in the far corner opens and Kassri walks back into the room, *Oh no, it's my turn.* Cold sweat trickles down her back unable to move a muscle. Kassri pushes her into the inner courtyard moving her fleetingly past the fountain that trickles gently between lush green plants with tiny pink and blue blooms and a fragrance so soft, it is breathtaking. Beyond the courtyard takes them back into the house and down a corridor that rattles with the woman's screams that fire their engines before reducing to a whimper. A door is ajar and Sarah stops to investigate the terror that someone is suffering. A woman lies face down along an enormous red couch. Her yellow embroidered dress, fans out and covers her feet.

'That's my daughter Jameela. Leave her,' says Kassri.

Michelle Hockley

'Are you crazy? You can't leave anyone in this much pain. Where's her mother?'

'She has no mother. She has only me.'

'You can't leave someone alone in this state.'

'There is nothing we can do, her life is ruined.'

'Her life ruined? It sounds to me like she needs a doctor. Get her a doctor.'

Taking Kassri by surprise, perhaps a moment of weakness as he looks upon his daughter in such distress, Sarah manages to free herself from his hold and goes to kneel beside the couch. 'Do you need a doctor? Please look at me. Talk to me if you can.'

The woman of about 20 years old, lifts her head; eyes full of tears but she doesn't speak and falls straight back onto the couch sobbing. Sarah rubs the girls back and starts to feel a stillness.

'Come now young lady, how can we help?' says Sarah.

'No one can help me. Mr Dowling has brought shame on me and my family. He has ruined my life.'

'Mr Dowling, you say? You know a Mr Peter Dowling?' enquires Sarah, completely taken aback.

'He has brought my family into disrepute. We shall never recover, from this.'

Kassri clicks his fingers. Two, much larger Arabs arrive out of nowhere and pull Sarah away from the scene; tossing her, like an unwanted slipper, into the corridor. Her motion stops dead with a thud against the wall. The two henchmen grab each end of Sarah; arms and legs between them, her handbag twisting and bouncing on the floor as she is carried out into the garden. With two or three swings that gain momentum, she is launched upwards and lands with an almighty bang alongside the calm and orderly swimming pool that is surrounded by a formation of unoccupied sun-lounges over looked by the Atlas mountains. *What is this place*, she thinks, *some sort of masochistic spar?* Kassri clicks his fingers again and his henchmen fall into place; lifting her up by the back of her collar and depositing her outside a stone towered annex at the north end of the garden. Another finger click from Kassri, and his sidekicks are gone, leaving Sarah short-winded. Kassri unlocks a heavy wooden door and shoves her inside where the scent of orange blossom oil fills the air.

'You won't get away with this,' says Sarah.

Another shunt and she is scaling the twisted staircase; Kassri close behind. Narrow slits along the tower wall appear at intervals; large enough for a sniper and adequate to peer through. As the heat racks up and they climb ever further, she stops a moment to catch her breath and takes a furtive look outside. The swimming pool, still unoccupied, waits tranquil, far in the distance and just a fraction of its size. Sweat runs down Henderson's face, her breathing is shallow and her muscles shake. Kassri squeezes past to unlock another heavy door. Light floods the room and Sarah shields her eyes. 'It's Mr Dowling,' she says seeing him sitting in the far corner with his back against the wall. For a brief second she thinks Kassri has brought her to collect Dowling, until her feet leave the floor and she is catapulted inside the room sinking into the cushions that dress a divan. Clambering upright, tangled in the cloth, she hears the door slam shut and the key turn. Getting to her feet she rushes to the door and thumps ferociously. But there is barely a sound from the dense wood that holds firm against its frame. With her ear pressed tightly on the solid door she hears a sunken empty sound of footsteps reverberating back to her. As another heavy door closes and locks, Kassri leaves the building and she knows she's beaten. Exhausted, head thumping, Sarah slides down to the polished floor and turns to the abductee. The aroma of orange blossom continues its presence creating a freshness in what might otherwise be a pleasant and pretty room.

'Mr Dowling,' says Sarah, out of breath. 'I'm DC Henderson, Metropolitan Police,' tapping her pockets in an attempt to locate her badge.

Mr Dowling scrambles quickly to his feet but his legs give way. On all fours, he crawls closer to the wall hoping to guide himself to the door. 'Someone. Anyone, please. Help me. I'm hallucinating.'

Art For Art's Sake

'You are not hallucinating Mr Dowling,' says Sarah moving quickly towards him, taking out a tissue to mop the moisture from his face. She dabs his temples and passes him a glass of water from the jug on the table next to the daybed. Dowling sits with his back firmly against the wall; his arms tight around his legs and chin balancing on his knees.

'How did you get here?' asks Dowling. 'How did you find me?'

'Not now, Mr Dowling. You are in a lot of trouble and it would seem, so am I. What have you done to that poor young woman?'

'There's been a terrible mistake,' he says as he releases a tightly clenched hand to thump the floor; screwing up his face as tears start to fall.

'Come now Mr Dowling. Please, sip some more water,' says Sarah, picking up the glass to encourage him to drink. 'You've had a terrible shock. Let us take a moment to calm ourselves so we can think.'

Sarah removes her black court shoes to sit more comfortably on her knees; sighting Dowling wearing his moccasin slippers somewhat dusty and dishevelled.

'They've got it all wrong,' pleads Peter.

'Well, as far as I'm concerned,' starts DC Henderson, 'this whole situation is looking incredibly fishy to me. You won't believe who accosted me before those thugs arrived and brought me here. I bet you can't guess,' says Sarah, wanting somehow to lighten Dowling's load.

'I can guess,' replies Dowling.

'Who then?' says Sarah.

'Cedric Carlton-Smyth?'

'Blimey, how did you get that?'

'He piloted the plane that brought me here.'

'What? Does he have a pilot's licence? Is he qualified to fly passengers?'

'You are missing the point. It's not the number of flying hours that you need to worry about it's the fact he's co-operating with this Arab family; leading them to me and landing the blame firmly at my door.'

'Well, you are wrong about flying hours, Mr Dowling,'

'Am I?'

'Yes, you are. Anyone knows that to fly passengers, you need the correct number of flying hours to be awarded the licence.'

Dowling puts his head back into his knees and rests his head as he tries to explain. 'I think Carlton-Smyth must be into something pretty deep and using anyone and doing anything to take the heat off himself?'

'No that can't be right. I'm talking about Cedric Carlton-Smyth who set up the research project that we both worked on at *The British Archives* for the Foreign and Commonwealth team.'

'Exactly. Yes, the very same Cedric Carlton-Smyth.'

'But he can't fly a plane.'

'Stop going on about flying. It's the same Carlton-Smyth. The one who asked us, over ten years ago, to analyse data...'

'... regarding trade routes,' interrupts Sarah, 'that went in and out of Morocco before and after the independence from France in 1956.'

'Yes, well remembered after so long ago.'

'Nothing wrong with my memory Mr Dowling. Please do continue.'

'Well, as you know, those particular trade documents referred to a specific demographic, and when they came into the public domain, were highly sought after. Everyone wanted a piece of them.'

'Yes, I remember. This was also the first time I met Mr Carlton-Smyth.'

'Yes, he was paying for the research. It wasn't coming out of the Treasury budget, so he could request his own team. He asked specifically for me to be on the project and I asked for you to join the work. It was just us who were working on those documents.'

'Go on,' says Sarah.

'Well, as you also know, that research exposed Moroccan families who were starting to gain ground on their trading capabilities; becoming rather more successful than their counterparts. This period in history was when some families saw an opportunity to reinvent themselves; move themselves through the ranks of society.

'Nothing wrong with that,' replies Sarah.

'No, but it raised a lot of questions and a lot of eyebrows among the noble families and ruling classes.'

'I was particularly interested in a Thorfa Kassri,' says Sarah.

'Well, you might also be interested to know that Thorfa Kassri's grandson, Jamal Kassri, is the man who has locked you in this room,' replies Peter.

'What? No?'

'Oh yes. The thug who stuck a pistol in the nape of my neck is his grandson.'

'Well, I'll be damned. When I heard the name Kassri at the airport yesterday, it made me think for a second, but I passed it off as a common name in this area. He owns the private jet that brought you here.'

'I don't doubt it.'

'And his sidekick was bloody rough when he gagged me with your curtain ties.'

'My curtains? What's happened to them?'

'Nothing and if you can be bothered about curtain ties, Mr Dowling, at a time like this, you must be starting to feel a little more yourself,' says Sarah.

'No. it is just that...'

Art For Art's Sake

'...Mr Dowling,' jumps in Sarah, anxious to make sense of their plight. 'So is all this aggression towards us because of that research project? Am I here because I tried to investigate the reason for the Kassri family's social climb? I remember, just as I was getting somewhere, bang...'

'...the project was abruptly halted and all the documents along with our research, disappeared,' interjects Dowling.

'What do you mean, disappeared?' repeats Sarah.

'Yes. You won't find that research anywhere.'

'But the documents are in the public domain. Anyone can read them.'

'Not any more they're not. If you tried to find them in the *The British Archives'* catalogue, you won't find a trace.'

'You've got me thinking about that project,' says Sarah, 'I was really getting somewhere with Thorfa Kassri. It's coming back to me. He was a descendant of the Ladris family line; an early aristocratic Muslim family in Morocco, ninth century, they'd previously lost most of their wealth and was now, in the 1950s gaining traction.'

'Yes, that's right.'

'...and on the limited evidence available to us, especially when the documents were removed, we concluded that the wealth of these so called upstarts, had always been present and it was the tide of the economy that caused a fluctuation in prospects,' adds Sarah.

'Yes, as simple as that.'

'So, did you try to find the documents again after the project was dissolved?' asks Sarah.

'Not then, but recently I have and to my surprise, they've gone, vanished,' says Dowling stretching out his legs, pulling a painful expression as his muscles unfurl.

'Go on, Mr Dowling, I'm all ears.'

'I do lots of research for Carlton-Smyth, he has some very wealthy clients who request him to find unusual pieces of art.'

'Oh that's interesting.'

'Yes, it is. Well it was, until now.'

'What did he ask you to find?' says Sarah.

'He had a request from a Moulay Arif Salamine, asking to find what he could about a seventeenth century female family member of the Kassri family, a descendant of the Ladris family, twelfth generation. It sounded interesting when Smyth asked me to get involved.'

'That is the same family who we found in the project at *The British Archives?*'

'Yes, that's right.'

'So what did you find this time? Don't tell me. Another forbidden document?'

'No. A beautiful miniature painting of Kassri's grandmother from the 1600s.'

Art For Art's Sake

'Where did you find that?'

'*Yates Gallery*, in Hull. At first I wasn't sure I'd found the right family member, because the painting is of a European lady with an English name. I have since confirmed my findings with other documents.'

'You always were thorough with your research.'

'Yes, and finding the marriage in a parish record in Kent, was a real hallelujah moment.'

'Oh, how intriguing,' says Sarah, taking a seat in a wicker chair, hugging a cushion and making herself comfortable.

'I informed Cedric of my findings and he almost bit my hand off. Negotiations to purchase from the gallery got underway immediately. The next thing, Smyth's giving me instructions to collect the item from the gallery and deliver to the flower girl on the Pimlico Market, Chelsea, London.'

'He asked you to deliver to your niece? DS Trait?'

'Who? I don't have a niece and I certainly don't know a DS Trait. Who's that?'

'The woman in your sitting room, when I arrived at your house.'

'No. That's not right. Carlton-Smyth didn't mention anything about a police officer and anyway, I saw her quite a few times on the market selling flowers before I was ready to deliver.'

'Didn't you think it odd, leaving a piece of art

with someone selling flowers?'

'I did think it a little odd. I usually just give the items to Smyth, but he made different arrangements this time because he was going to be away,' replies Dowling.

'Getting back to your research. Did you ever find out why our project was shut down so abruptly?'

'No and I never asked Cedric. I mean that was a decade ago.'

'So who are the Salamines?'

They are a noble family. In fact these two families; the Kassris and the Salamines are rivals. They've been enemies for hundreds of years.'

'Why are the Salamines interested in Kassri's grandmother of four hundred years ago?'

'Well, I've since learnt, that the eldest son of the Salamine family has fallen in love with Jameela, Kassri's daughter. The Salamine family, it would seem, intend to find anything they can to stop the marriage going ahead.'

'And they think, with the Kassris being descendants of a European, it is reason enough to stop a marriage?'

'Well yes. It's not pure Arab is it?'

'That is madness. Surely none of us can be that pure. Haven't we all got a little of something else in our DNA?'

'It might not be important to us or to anyone else, but it seems it is important to the Kassri and the

Salamine family.'

'Why am I here? What have I got to do with all of this?'

'I guess, because your name appears alongside mine, on the repository register at *The British Archives*, as taking out associated documents. You were part of the original project.'

'But those documents were nothing to do with Kassri's DNA,' says Sarah.

'No, but there must have been something untoward in those documents, given the speed it was closed down.'

'And we never got the chance to find it.'

'No. That is one that got away,' says Dowling.

'So, I wonder if Kassri believes I have exposed his family's wealth as coming from European descent?'

'He might do,' replies Dowling.

'But I didn't find evidence of that. I never got the chance.'

'They don't know that. They don't know how far you got into the documents that might destroy their reputation and the opportunity to marry into a higher social status.'

'My goodness, this is crazy. Archivists being locked up for their research,' replies Sarah.

'Well, I'm not sure it's so unusual nowadays.'

'For me it is. It was over a decade ago and well, I

never found anything damning on their family. Why now? Why not ten years ago or eight or seven?'

'The prospect of a marriage into a noble family has triggered this.'

'So why didn't they take me from your house? Two birds and one stone.'

'They didn't know you were Sarah Henderson from *The British Archives.'*

'So, how did they find out? More intriguingly, how did they know I was in Marrakesh?'

'I think it was after we landed in Morocco. Smyth got a telephone call. He was talking to someone a, Mango or Mungo? I heard your name when Smyth and Kassri were shouting at each other with erratic arm gestures. I wondered if they'd hurt you, or even worse, after I left the house.'

'Who did you say Smyth was talking to?'

'I couldn't be sure. I felt so groggy after that flight. They injected me with drugs you know.'

'I didn't know,' replies Sarah, pausing only long enough to show some sympathy to Peter, before starting up again. 'Mr Dowling, try and think who was on the telephone to Smyth,' she says.

'The only name mentioned, was Mungo...or Mango. A Matron Mango. I don't know, sorry.'

'Malcolm Monroe,' says Sarah in a loud whisper.

'Who's Malcolm Monroe?'

Art For Art's Sake

'He's Chief Inspector at Blythe Street Police Station. We left Monroe with instructions to request you and your captors be detained at Marrakesh airport.'

'So how is it that we were not detained at the airport?' asks Dowling.

'I don't know. None of this makes any sense. I mean, take the Salamines. If it was so important for them to maintain their pure Arab breeding, or to find the evidence they needed to stop the wedding, why didn't they just ask Jameela to take a DNA test. After all, who can argue with science?'

'It was only a rumour, they had no proof of there being European DNA in the Kassri family. It was bordering on a myth because it was such an old tale. I personally think it was rather clever of the Salamines to try to squash or unearth the rumour in this way. Much more classy than asking someone to steel Jameela's hair brush?'

'It has a certain ring to it. I give it that.'

'Don't mock the Salamine family. This way is far more honourable and they truly believed this was enough to halt the wedding.'

'Things still don't add up to me. I mean, how did Kassri even know the research was being undertaken? Let alone that an incriminating piece of evidence had been found?'

'That is something I've been thinking about for

the past twenty plus hours. Do you think it's possible Kassri has placed a request with all UK archives, asking to be notified when anything is found about his family?'

'Well, it's not beyond the pale. When you have money like the Kassri family, pretty much anything is possible for the right price.'

'It must be easy to instigate, it's just intelligence gathering.'

'I'm intelligence gathering Mr Dowling. So, do you know why Carlton-Smyth is helping Kassri after being employed by the Salamines?'

'Well we both know that Kassri is not the type of person who reasons with you. There is no room for negotiation, so maybe Smyth had no choice. Maybe there was a gun in the nape of his neck too.'

'Maybe, but now he is free; allowed to wander the streets of Marrakesh while we are held captive?' says Sarah.

'We don't know that he is free. It sounds like he led Kassri to you and, well who knows where he is now.'

'Probably on a plane heading to Blighty I shouldn't wonder. I know of at least one spare seat on a flight.'

'You don't know that Sarah,' says, Dowling.

'Can I remind you, Mr Dowling, that you need to address me as DC Henderson.'

'Really?'

'It is much better that way, more professional with me being a member of the Metropolitan Police.'

'Thank you for reminding me of your profession, DC Henderson. Since that is the case, and you've doubtlessly been tasked with returning the abductee safely to the UK, may I enquire as to how you are proposing to fulfil that duty?' he says, more than keen to hear Sarah's proposal, being pretty certain by now, that she hasn't any idea.

Sarah pulls a couple of sheets from the daybed and throws them to Dowling, partially landing over his head.

'What is this for?' he says, scrambling to free himself.

'Tie a knot. Tie them together,' says Sarah.

'And what do you intend on doing with this?' says Peter, holding up the sheets. 'Do you intend on climbing out of that window?' He says mockingly.

'Mr Dowling, please, a firm knot,' replies Sarah stretching up with the full length of a sheet, trying to find the end.

'If you say so,' says Peter.

'Can we refocus on the miniature painting, which I am thinking, is what Kassri took from the desk in your study?'

'Yes, that is right.'

'So have I got this right, Mr Dowling? The son of

the Salamines, a rival family of the Kassri family, falls in love with Jameela, the daughter of Jamal Kassri and proposes marriage?'

'Yes,' says Peter, 'though when I was asked to find evidence, I wasn't told it was proof enough to halt the marriage of two people who'd fallen in love.'

'No, I'm quite sure that wasn't your intention.'

'My aim in research is for people to understand the past, not to ruin someone's future.'

'But there is something that I still can't square, Mr Dowling.'

'Oh no. You always were a dog with a bone when it came to facts. Go on.'

'Who else in this lineage is showing European characteristics in their DNA? Someone must have exhibited something during the past four hundred years? How have they fared? Or, were they locked in a cell, away from prying eyes? Disowned. Shamed,' says Sarah as if performing a soliloquy in a Shakespeare play as she hams up what she considers to be a ridiculous family feud.

'There is no one with European DNA in the Kassri family resulting from this particular branch of the family,' says Peter.

'Are you saying, the rumour, that has circulated for four hundred years, even with evidence of the miniature portrait, is unfounded?' says Sarah.

'Yes, that is what I'm saying.'

'How can you be so sure without looking at all subsequent family members; checking each of their appearances. It's impossible. The only reliable method is to check Jameela's own DNA.'

'I didn't need to. My findings show clearly that the grandmother was a step-mother, and whilst she looked after the family, she bore no children of her own that entered the Kassri family line of descent. All children that proceed in the family line are all accounted for and stem from the previous mother before this woman arrived on the scene.'

'Ah...! Which is why the family have managed to suppress the European gene for 400 years; there isn't one. Oh my Lord. Have you told Kassri and Jameela what you have told me?'

'No, I haven't told anyone. I mean, it took me a while to work out why they were so upset and I've never been given the chance to explain,' replies Dowling as Sarah starts to pull her phone from inside her jacket pocket.

'Damn no signal. We have to get this information to the Kassri family. They are silencing us to protect their reputation. When they kill us, which they will have no qualms about doing, then their job is done. They can easily bury us somewhere on this beautiful estate or beneath those stunning Atlas mountains,' says Sarah, looking out of the window and down to the ground, being reminded of how far up they are.

She looks around the room and up to the ceiling for an obvious exit, muttering, 'how dare they drag you out of your home at gun point and put us both in a turret because a family member might be of a different race. I refuse to play these archaic games. Who cares what colour anyone is? If the off spring is healthy, isn't that enough?'

'That might be your liberal view but it's not that of the Salamine and Kassri family. I'd have thought that was evident, given where we are now.'

'You're starting to sound like a Nazi, making excuses for proposing an Aryan society and quite frankly, that doesn't suit you Mr Dowling.'

'I don't agree with insisting on pure breeding but we have to understand that these families date back hundreds of years. They have a different outlook on life. You can't knock their beliefs just because they don't align with your own ethics. Can't you at least see this from their point of view?'

'Yes, sure, if I wasn't being treated so cruelly, having been caught up in their need for purity in descent which, incidently, is causing great unhappiness to their children.'

'Well it's not all about you,' replies Dowling, annoyed by Sarah's intolerant remarks and inflexibility to see both sides of the debate.

'Well, if you ask me,' starts Sarah, pulling more sheets and blankets off the daybed and tossing the cushions in the far corner, 'Jameela has had a lucky escape from such a small minded, petty family as the Salamines,' standing now, knee deep in cloth, still pulling in a slightly frenzied manner.

'What are you doing, Sarah?'

'Erm...DC Henderson,' says Sarah.

'What are you doing, DC Henderson?'

'Take hold of that end, Mr Dowling,' throwing another sheet to him.

'Are you mad?'

'Yes if I stay here any longer I'm mad,' she replies, continuing to pull off all the bedclothes and tying a knot between anything she finds; blankets, throws and towels.

'Who do you think you are? King Charles I, trying to escape from Carisbrooke Castle?' says Peter.

'Well, if I do, I shall be a darn sight more successful than that futile attempt of an escape,' says Sarah, though in reality her courage for leaving her prison cell, via a makeshift ladder, is being driven by anger; aware that if she over thinks what she is doing, it will result in nothing more than a lot of hot-air. *Don't think Sarah, just do,* enjoying the fire raging in her belly, sniggering on hearing Peter's comments about Charles I's escape. *Once a historian, always a historian and a right wing historian to boot.*

'Still not a royalist then?' adds Peter

Peter can't believe his eyes, watching her pulling at the sheets and tying a series of knots, as he waits patiently for the melodrama to subside. He isn't alarmed because he's quite certain he is never going to agree to trust her knots and wouldn't want her to trust them either.

'Don't do this DC Henderson. They will shoot you down before you get to the ground.'

'It is not just me they will shoot at, you are coming too. And we are both taking this chance.'

'Not before we try to get their attention by shouting out of the window. Someone will come to us.'

Sarah knows it makes sense to leave via the door rather than being shot at whilst scaling the wall of the tower, *though think of the headlines.*

'Okay, you might be right, Mr Dowling,' she says perching herself on the side of the daybed; clutching the sheet that she is in the process of binding. She feels the wind leave her inflated sails and former strength and determination quickly recede. The rage inside her ebbs allowing for her negativity to flow freely. 'Okay Mr Dowling, you are probably right. What do you want to shout then?' ask Sarah.

'I shall leave that to you,' replies Peter.

'What about, help? That seems to be the common

term for such a situation.'

'Yes, it always worked when Lassie was in the vicinity or that Kangaroo, whatever was his name?'

'Skippy.'

'Yes, that's right. Skippy the bush kangaroo,' says Peter, somewhat pleased with himself for such a suggestion.

'Shall we start to shout then? You go first,' says Sarah.

'You should go first. You are Metropolitan police.'

Sarah's frustration returns bringing with it anger and rage once more. She ignores Dowling and instead, gathers up the sheets that are splayed across the floor and on finding one end of the cloth, ties it to the leg of the day bed; throwing the other end towards the window.

'You are not serious are you?' asks Dowling.

'Yes, I am. Come on. You first,' making the mistake of looking out the window. 'Heavens, that is a long way down, Mr Dowling.'

'I know it is. You have lost your mind.'

'You will be fine,' says Sarah chucking the bed sheets out of the window making a trail down the side of the building and demonstrating the type of technique he needs to adopt with his feet and hands.

'Really? Well, if I'm shot at, on your head be it. This is preposterous, putting a British civilian in danger like this. It is an outrage. Didn't they teach you anything at police school.'

'Police school what's that?'

'I knew it. You are missing some vital training.'

'I'm still in training. I'm on probation.'

'Oh great, that explains a lot.'

Shut up Mr Dowling. Window. Now.'

'Gosh you are bossy.'

'Not as bossy as your niece, I can assure you of that.'

'How many more times? I don't have a niece.'

'Whatever. Now, do you need me to help you up to the window frame?'

Peter doesn't reply. Instead, reluctantly and somewhat clumsily, takes a stance to prepare himself to exit the window.

'The sheets don't reach the ground by a long way,' notes Mr Dowling.

'No, so prepare yourself to jump the final part.'

Sarah can't tell if Peter heard that last instruction or not. He hasn't responded and the concentration on his face is, to all intents and purposes, quite painful to watch. His slippers push him off from the sill, giving him the momentum he needs. In using the technique Sarah gave him to bounce off the wall at intervals, allows him to be guided down the length of the bedsheets. Sarah peers out of the window and sees Peter grabbing the sheet for his life; looking as white as the makeshift ladder he is holding. The daybed shunts towards the window inside the room, Sarah prays the knots hold fast. She hears him jump the last part, landing on the ground below with a thud and a wilting screech.

That is one down, one to go, thinks Sarah, also feeling ill-at-ease to be abseiling from such an uncomfortable height. Stuffing her shoes into her jacket pocket and swivelling her handbag on her shoulder she then checks the knot around the daybed. *Fortunately,* she thinks, *Peter is a lightweight so hopefully those knots that drape the side of the building, haven't suffered too much strain.* As she lowers herself, keeping calm and focused, the ground soon nears and she knows at that point, if the sheet gives way, she can easily jump from here with a minor break. At the final push away from the wall, she swings outwards and jumps to meet the ground.

'I don't quite know how, but we made it,' says Peter, still out of breath and shuffling from foot to foot as he holds out a hand for Sarah to balance whilst she puts her shoes back on.

The swimming pool remains undisturbed as they walk along the edges, back towards the house, all the while looking for an opening in the fence that can lead them out from the grounds and back onto the street.

'Where are you going?' whispers Peter, crouching forward; taking long strides in a stealth like fashion, looking not too dissimilar to the Pink Panther as he files in behind Sarah.

'What do you mean?' whispers Sarah.

'We need to explain ourselves, otherwise we'll be looking over our shoulder for the rest of our lives.'

'We are not walking straight into the Lion's den after risking life and limb. We shall explain, but at a safe distance when we return to London.'

'Sabah alkhyr.' Good morning, says a gardener appearing abruptly from a rather lush looking flower bed.

Sarah yelps and Peter squeals as he clings to her shoulder. He wonders, not for the first time, why she ever chose the police as a profession, given her limited observation skills. The gardener, keeping hold of his rake, moves towards them.

'Please,' starts the gardener,' je vous emmène à la maison pour rencontrer Monsieur Kassri. Please come.' I take you to the house to meet Mr. Kassri.

'Ignore him Mr Dowling,' says Sarah, pulling at Peter's arm to get him away from the gardener and continue with their escape.

'Ouch that's my arm?' says Peter.

'Well come along then. Quick,' mutters Sarah to Dowling before calling back to the gardener. 'We are fine, merci. We are leaving now. Is this the way out? Sortie?' says Sarah, pointing to the far corner as she starts to make long strides away from him.

'Par ici,' replies the gardener. This way, indicating to the main house with a broad smile.

'Thank you,' says Peter to the gardener, pulling away from Sarah.

'No Mr Dowling,' shouts Sarah, tugging him back. 'That will take us to the house.'

Another squeal from Peter causes Sarah to turn towards him and sees, standing alongside the gardener, Kassri and Nader.

'My gardener is quite right,' says Kassri. 'Please, this way,' gesturing towards the door that Sarah recognises from a horizontal position when thrown from the house to land at the side of the swimming pool.

Sarah and Peter look briefly at each other before turning towards the two men standing ahead of them. Sarah and Peter reluctantly shuffle closer towards their captors.

'Please don't look so surprised Mr Dowling,' says Kassri. 'We've heard your explanation. You don't think for a moment we left you in the annex without surveillance do you? What a wasted opportunity that would have been,' chuckles Kassri. 'Come now, this way,' repeats Kassri directing them both inside the house.

With a noticeable absence of pushing, shoving, guns or force, Sarah and Peter stand on the threshold to where Jameela lies sleeping. She rests quietly. Seemingly cherished by the opulence of her surroundings decorated with an abundance of heavy fabrics adorning the alcoves of this grand hall of intimate holdings. She catches sight of Mr Dowling and the spell of stillness is at once broken.

'Get out of here,' shouts Jameela, pointing to Peter. 'How dare you set your eyes upon me. I, who is destroyed by your actions. Get out of here.'

Peter physically withdraws on hearing the harsh shrill in her voice, but in doing so meets eye to eye with Kassri who immediately encourages him to enter further into the room with a firm hand on his shoulder.

'Jameela, my dear,' says her father. 'Mr Dowling has something to tell you, something that makes us all very happy.'

'I will not listen to him father,' replies Jameela.

'Mr Dowling, tell Jameela what you have been telling Miss Henderson whilst you were in my annex.'

'It's not Miss. It is DC Henderson,' announces Sarah, which Kassri immediately ignores and to which Peter shudders at the inconsequential need for Henderson to insist on her correct title.

'Mr Dowling,' starts Kassri. 'Please, my daughter is waiting.'

Peter's legs begin to shake, not least because of the *bungee jump,* and asks if he might sit down. With a nod from Jameela, Sarah and Peter synchronise their movements to the sage-green leather pouffes from where Peter begins to make amends.

'Art of this delicacy,' starts Peter, 'of this rarity and fineness, should be seen as an object of beauty. The miniature portrait was never painted with the intention of one day bringing shame upon your family or to destroy your future happiness.'

'Why couldn't you have left our family secret hidden?' replies Jameela. 'Why did it have to be exposed in this way?'

'It was not of my choosing, it was that of your future father-in-law; looking for a reason to halt your marriage,' adds Peter.

'Oh no,' wails Jameela. 'Please stop. I will not listen to you for a moment longer,' throwing herself once more onto the sofa.

Sarah glares at Peter, horrified by his lack of diplomacy in not making the slightest attempt to sugar coat the truth. *She doesn't need to know about the rarity of the art piece,* thinks Sarah, *and she certainly doesn't need to hear about the Salamine family disrupting her happiness. She just wants to know if she has a future.* Henderson leans towards Jameela to take the lead, hoping she might fare better in patching up the mess that Peter has seemingly caused. 'Please listen Jameela,' moving off the pouffe to sit beside her.

Peter sits perfectly still, somewhat in shock to see,

first hand, the devastation he has brought to a person through art; being almost more than his own heart can take. He waits patiently for a lull in the sobbing where he might continue to give counsel. He hears Jameela let out a sigh and Peter intercept the gap of emotion.

'Jameela, please listen to me,' he says. 'Your concerns, that you might carry the DNA of a European; proving your blood line to be impure, is very much mistaken. Your grandmother, of the seventeenth century, did not bear children.'

With her face reddened from the constant tears, Jameela slowly sits up; places her hands gently on her lap and makes her address.

'Are you saying, Mr Dowling, that I am not carrying the gene of a European? That neither myself nor my father are of European descent?'

'That's right. That is exactly what I am saying. The only misdemeanour committed is that your ancestor fell in love with a beautiful woman.'

Jameela starts to smile. Her eyes red and cheeks flushed. Peter feels himself responding with a smile too.

'Isn't that wonderful news Jameela' says Kassri. 'A rumour that has hung over our family for hundreds of years has been banished by this good man, Mr Dowling. We need worry no more that one day a Kassri might appear as a European.'

Sarah sits back onto the pouffe. Peter sees she is

noticeably biting her lip fighting back her opinionated rhetoric in defence that to be of European descent or of any other descent, is not abhorrent.

'I don't know how to thank you Mr Dowling,' says Jameela.

'Don't thank me,' replies Peter, standing up as she approaches. 'These are just the facts and well, I work better with facts,' *than whatever I've been going through for the past twenty four hours,* smiles Peter.

Kassri walks to the centre of the room and speaks to his daughter, asking her to go and wash her face.

'Yes father,' she replies politely, walking towards an adjoining room to make the necessary adjustments that have been requested of her.

Without the focus on Jameela, silence consumes the room and Peter wonders if Henderson might fill that void by suggesting they take their leave while Kassri's mood is more congenial. But no, nothing is forthcoming from her, and Kassri starts instead to address Mr Dowling.

'I've had your research verified at the *Yates Gallery* in Hull, and everything I heard you say to DC Henderson during your short stay here, checks out. I thank you for that, Mr Dowling.'

'Oh. Oh have you?' says Peter, not knowing quite what to make of what he's hearing. *One thing's for sure,* thinks Peter, *Kassri has the full co-operation of the Yates*

Gallery. I wonder if indeed he does have an alarm set on requests made for documents relevant to himself? Is that actually a thing? Peter knows there would be no value in retaliating or getting into conversation about how Kassri operates, instead, he turns to Henderson for support, but sees she's become distracted by an ornament on the side table.

'And, as it turns out, Mr Dowling,' continues Kassri, 'what I heard from you, and what has been confirmed, has saved you from further discomfort. Though you could have met a much worse fate when you chose to scale down my annex wall. That was very brave of you.'

Peter has neither the inclination nor the desire to say another word but on seeing Sarah admiring the art work at the far end of the room, he is left with no choice but to wait. *How is she a DC,* thinks Peter. *She hasn't got a clue. Why isn't she getting us away from here; out of the clutches of this family?*

'So, Mr Dowling,' starts Kassri. 'I have the object stowed away in my safe for my eyes only. This woman from the sixteen hundreds, can no longer bring shame upon my family.'

'But this woman in the miniature painting...' Peter stops himself, having run out of steam.

'...Yes, I know, I understand Mr Dowling. As I say, I heard everything in your explanation which has been confirmed, and I am very grateful for your honest account. I am somewhat embarrassed by the stress I have caused you, but you must understand, I shall do anything for my daughter. Anything.'

It would seem that way, thinks Peter. *The indignation of anyone to assume it acceptable to steal another person's property; a notion that has not even crossed this person's mind.*

'I see it in your eyes, Mr Dowling. You are worried that I have stolen the art from the Salamine family.'

Peter maintains a smile as his thoughts continue. *Well you have stolen a piece of art, but don't mind me. You carry on. Do what you want. You seem to anyway. And well, we have a member of the Met Police over there admiring your art work, and if she's not bothered by your antics, then quite frankly, why should I?*

'You worry too much, Mr Dowling. You are forgetting the miniature painting is of my family and therefore it belongs to me.'

Your interpretation of property ownership is not strictly true is it? A fabrication to suit your own ends, which by your standards is fine. How do you sleep at night? thinks Peter.

Feeling more and more uncomfortable in Kassri's company, Dowling pinches the side of his leg hoping to stabilise the frustration mounting inside him each time

Kassri opens his mouth. He is relieved when Jameela returns, bursting back into the room, causing the atmosphere to up its tempo.

'Papa, can we at least invite these good people to take a meal with us?' asks Jameela bounding up to her father, leaving a fragrant trail of freshly picked rose petals.

Peter can't believe what he's hearing. *To partake in a meal with an abductor? No thank you. Break bread with him. No thank you. I applaud you for the lengths you are prepared to go for your daughter, but what about everyone else and all the other rules you are breaking? One thing is certain, I don't have Stockholm Syndrome,* thinks Peter, causing himself to titter under his breath whilst maintaining the smile that is now firmly fixed.

'Thank you,' says DC Henderson, returning to join the group and looking directly at Kassri with a grin from ear to ear. 'Refreshments of sorts will be wonderful, thank you. First though, might I use your bathroom, I feel awfully grubby after our ordeal.'

No Henderson. Please no. thinks Peter with an almost constipated appearance; feeling bruised, tired and just wanting to leave this establishment.

'Jameela will direct you,' replies Kassri swishing his arm to command his daughter into action.

On arriving at the bathroom, Henderson thanks Jameela for escorting her and the instant the door closes, turns on the tap in the tiny sink and runs the water. Leaning with her back against the door she takes out her phone and scrolls down to find the text she sent while looking at the art on the wall at the far end of the room. Seeing that she hasn't received a reply, starts to type another text; her hands shake as the water dances in the basin.

```
Chief Superintendent.
Now would be a good time. Now...!
```

'Are you alright in there?' calls out Jameela.

'Yes, very fine thank you,' replies Henderson, a little flustered, putting away the phone, buckling up her handbag and taking a quick glance in the mirror. *My goodness, I look terrible. It's after looking at the beautiful Jameela,* she thinks. *Oh youth... it is such a valuable commodity.*

'I was getting worried,' says Jameela as Henderson opens the door.

'I'm sorry for taking so long, Jameela. You didn't need to wait.'

As Henderson walks beside Jameela, so small in frame, delicate, fragile, and smiling in such a jolly fashion, she feels a pang of guilt for calling the chief to make an arrest; leaving Jameela without a father to care for her whilst he's serving time in prison.

On re-entering the grand room, where Kassri and

Peter are seemingly waiting on her return, Sarah positions herself between them and forges an appearance that might adequately veil her recent actions. Nader appears at the door. Sarah decides he's the tougher of the two captors; seeing herself being chucked about in Dowling's study. She watches him approach Kassri and hand him a bag; which Sarah identifies as a burgundy Armani document carrier.

Kassri turns to Sarah. 'This belongs to Mr Carlton-Smyth,' he says. 'I doubt, after failing to bring you to us, he will return, and we certainly have no further need for his co-operation.'

'What do you suppose I want with Mr Carlton-Smyth's belongings?' ask Sarah abruptly, leaving the bag suspended mid-way between her and Kassri.

'You are police, are you not?' says Kassri. 'You are an authority in England and I presume you will be returning to the UK. Might you be responsible for one of your own citizen's belongings?'

'Yes. Thank you I shall ensure Mr Carlton-Smyth is returned his property,' replies Sarah acknowledging her short fall; feeling somewhat sheepish for her lack of authority to protect the property of a British national. *Jeeze, I'm useless.*

The maid, who had earlier presented Sarah so eloquently with mint tea, enters room and hands Kassri an envelope which he takes from her, reads the contents, then makes a sharp exit. Sarah walks across the room and peers out of the window, her emotions laying somewhere between thankful and awkward on seeing two stationary white 4x4s with the logo *Surété Nationale* blazoned along the side; standing in complete silence with their blue lights flashing. *Gosh, NCA and their counterparts abroad sure are efficient. They've wasted no time in tracking us down.*

Turning away from the window she sees Kassri return to the room between two Moroccan police officers. Jameela rushes to her father; throwing her arms around him in a tight embrace as four more officers enter and decorate the outer edges of the room.

'Oh father, this is all my fault.'

'No, Jameela, this is not your fault. I shall return very quickly. Please, I want you to stay with Nattier,' pointing to the maid.

Jameela releases her hold and glares directly at Mr Dowling leaving him in no doubt that she has returned the blame firmly back at his door.

Kassri leaves the room without a struggle. Nader follows behind between two more officers and Jameela and Nattier complete the procession in a sombre stride. The remaining two officers stand firm; one resting his right hand on his holstered weaponry, the other officer poised with his hands on broad hips. Sarah moves towards them.

'Good day,' she says, holding out her hand. 'I am DC Henderson, Metropolitan Police,' tapping her pocket but noticeably failing to locate her badge.

'Good day,' replies the officer. We apologise for the suffering that Mr Kassri has caused you both. We aim for your swift return to the UK once we have taken your statement.

Sarah turns to look at Peter Dowling, who by now appears lucid and frail. 'Are you okay, Mr Dowling,' she asks.

'Yes. But no statement,' says Peter in a weak and feeble voice.

'Mr Dowling?' says Sarah kneeling down beside him as he grips the edge of the seat that is set perfectly against the wall. 'You need to make a statement,' she whispers.

'Why? I just want to go home.'

'You want to press charges, don't you? You've been through an horrific ordeal.'

Sarah kneels beside Mr Dowling and turns to the officers, 'can you give us a minute please?' They nod their heads and step outside; leaving Sarah and Peter alone.

'Mr Dowling. What are you thinking? You must give a statement.'

'I can't talk here,' says Peter.

'Why ever not?' asks Sarah.

'Kassri has this place bugged. Didn't you hear him? He's had all my research checked while we were in the tower room. He knew what we were talking about.'

'Yes, I heard Kassri say that. But we have the police here to protect us and Kassri and Nader are on their way to the police station. You are not in any danger. Not now.'

'What is the point of making a statement?' says Dowling in a whisper that's now barely audible.

'So you can press charges and get justice. That is the point.'

'If I don't press charges will that be the end of it? I don't want years of waiting for a court case and having to give evidence. I want my life back. I want to forget about all of this?'

'It is not my decision to make Mr Dowling, but I would strongly advise you to get justice.'

'These things take years to come to court. I'd be hounded by the press or the police with more questions. I just want to go back to normal. Rewind the last twenty four hours.'

'Mr Dowling. Not so fast. After all, Kassri drugged you, abducted you, stole property from your home and then proceeded to steal property from the Salamine family. Notwithstanding, throwing me into a Calèche and goodness knows what they did to Carlton-Smyth to make him fly a plane. People have served at

Her Majesty's pleasure for committing far less crime. This is big and Kassri should be banged to rights. I advise you therefore, Mr Dowling, to make a statement so you can press charges.'

'Shush. Keep your voice down,' starts Peter Dowling on seeing the police officers returning to the room.

'Okay,' whispers Sarah to Dowling, 'leave this with me. I shall take it from here.'

'No, wait,' says Peter, pulling Sarah back to his side. 'Kassri won't ever do this again. It's not like he's a member of a gang; people trafficking. He did this for the love of his daughter. That is all he ever wanted to do.'

'How do we know he's not in a gang? Or what more he's capable of?'

'I don't have the nerve to fight this man. I want out and to return to my quiet lifestyle. Let Kassri and the Salamines fight this out amongst themselves. It's feudal. It's rivalry.'

'It's barbaric,' adds Sarah.

'Okay, but I don't want to be involved with them, I want to forget about them.'

'Mr Dowling, you are making a huge mistake. I advise you to think about it very carefully,' replies Sarah.

'Do I have to make a decision now, as to whether I want this investigated?'

'No, you don't have to decide this instance,' says

Art For Art's Sake

Sarah.

Witnessing the final stages of this ordeal is a huge relief for both Sarah and Peter. Sarah picks up Carlton-Smyth's document case, swings her handbag around back into position and asks the police officers of the *Sûreté Nationale* to escort them both away from the house.

* * * * *

Coming into land at Heathrow airport, rain batters against the windows. Sarah smiles to herself as she and Mr Dowling make their final descent through thick, dense cloud, opening up to nothing more than a grey and overcast gloom; a sight that couldn't be more welcoming. She had already arranged for Peter's medical after such an ordeal and on making a statement, without yet pressing charges, he is now at liberty to return home. Knowing that he doesn't have to revisit Blythe Street Station to come face to face with the one-way mirror and brown Bakelite clock, is a relief to Dowling. But what neither of them know, as they disembark their flight, is that DS Anna-Belle Trait and Cedric Carlton-Smyth, who arrived from Marrakesh this morning and DCI Malcolm Monroe who arrived earlier today from The Bahamas, are being handcuffed by the Metropolitan Police and escorted to an awaiting squad car.

CHAPTER SIX

Calling Time

Sarah Henderson pulls out the chair from underneath her desk and takes a seat in the staff reading room at *The British Archives*.

'Your documents are ready for collection,' whispers a colleague, not wanting to disturb the other readers.

'Thank you,' she replies, grateful by how welcoming the staff have been on her return to rejoin the research team.

She feels a vibration in her pocket as her mobile phone alerts her to a call. Still unable to disassociate the telephone with a possible emergency that might require her immediate attention, she begins to answer as she makes her way out of the reading room.

'Hello Peter,' she whispers. 'Why are you disturbing me at work?'

'Can you get yourself to a Daily Telegraph? It's all over the papers,' replies Peter Dowling.

'Don't tell me, let me guess. The Tories have made further cuts and are slapping each other on their backs and giving out high fives?'

Peter chooses to ignore that comment, not wishing to get himself embroiled in a political spat today. 'I'm calling to let you know that the Old Bailey are close to returning a verdict. Details of the case has hit all the newspapers, so it will be in The Guardian as well.'

'Okay, got it,' replies Sarah, ending the conversation abruptly to make her way to the staff canteen where she is sure to find a newspaper, all be it by this time of day, out of sequence and slightly scrunched. On her way down the corridor she stops in her tracks on catching sight, through a half open door, a bank of CCTV monitors covering an entire wall of the Security Office and a wide screen television. *My goodness*, she thinks, surprised by what she sees. *All they had ten years ago was a friendly face dressed in a red jacket walking the floors, and a dusty old portable TV to inhibit the boredom because nothing ever happened. Now look at it!*

Head of Security catches sight of her and turns away from the screens.

'Hello Sarah, I'd heard you were back with us.'

'Hi Trevor,' she says, giving him a quick wave and a smile from the doorway, not wanting to cause any distraction from him standing guard over the documents. But as the sound of *Big Ben* booms out from the plasma screen to announce the lunchtime news, she pulls herself back and leans against the door frame to catch the headlines. The Old Bailey, in all its glory, appears on the TV. The newsreader swings her chair towards the live feed to bring what she describes, as a 'story we will not want to miss.'

'Good afternoon,' says the newsreader. 'We have Laura Teleosky, our Home Correspondent, joining us from outside the Old Bailey to bring us the latest on this extraordinary case. Hello Laura.'

'Good afternoon Katie,' says Laura, pushing her earpiece into her ear.

'I understand a guilty verdict has been reached and we are waiting to hear the judge's sentencing. As we wait, what more can you tell us as this incredible story unfolds?'

'*Guilty*,' whispers Sarah under her breath, her heart starting to gallop.

'Yes, an unbelievable heist, no other word for it,' begins Laura. 'We now know that a long-standing art expert of *Drakes*, the Auctioneers, a Mr Cedric Carlton-Smyth, circled the rich and famous, hovering in their orbit until he saw them ready to take his bait, at which time he'd swoop in for the prize, so to speak.'

Katie, the Newsreader, is left seemingly surprised by the bird of prey analogy, but then its what the BBC have come to expect from the lovely Laura.

'I might be playing devil's advocate here Laura, or showing my ignorance of such matters,' states Katie,

Michelle Hockley

'but what you have described so eloquently, is this not just a business transaction between those who want and those who can fulfil those desires?'

'Yes. But in walks a Detective Chief Inspector Malcolm Monroe of Blythe Street Police Station, Chelsea, and a Detective Sergeant Anna-Belle Trait, Metropolitan Covert Operations.'

'And the plot thickens, so to speak?' replies the Newsreader, shifting in her chair, beginning to relish being a part of the dialogue as this story unfolds.

'Yes indeed it does thicken, Katie.'

'So what more can you tell us?'

'The art expert, Mr Carlton-Smyth, employed notable researchers, all at the top of their game, to find these requested objects of art. All researchers, I might add, have been questioned and cleared of any wrongdoing.'

'So, the items requested by the clients were located by these researchers?'

'Yes, that's right. Once a price had been agreed with the vendor, Mr Cedric Carlton-Smyth arranged delivery.'

'That all sounds straight forward to me.'

'Not when I tell you that some of the items never arrived with the client but instead, diverted by Carlton-Smyth to a DS Trait who amongst many guises, was a flower seller on the Pimlico market, in Chelsea, London.'

'Sold flowers?' says Katie, screwing her face, having not seen that one coming. 'I thought you said she was a police officer.'

'Yes, that's right. DS Trait was moonlighting her covert skills.'

'Indeed so,' replies Katie slightly bemused. 'So,' she adds with some thrust, hoping to bring the report back on track. 'So, when the client didn't receive the item, it was missing from the moment it had been purchased,' reiterates Katie.

'Yes, you could say that, but it was formally noted as a lost item when DS Trait reported it stolen with the *Art and Antiques Unit* within the Metropolitan Police and details of it were added to the long list of items on the database.'

'Sorry, Laura,' says, Katie, 'you are starting to lose me now. So, when the item was diverted to either DS Trait, DCI Monroe or this person from *Drakes* the Auctioneers...'

'...Mr Carlton-Smyth,' adds Laura.

'Pardon?'

'The dealer from *Drakes*, his name is Mr Carlton-Smyth.'

'Oh yes, thank you. So, when the item failed to get to the client because it had been diverted to either one of Trait, Monroe or Carlton-Smyth, it was logged with the *Art and Antiques Unit* as , stolen.'

'Yes, that is right.'

'Why would they report the item missing when most probably it was entwined in a bouquet on the Pimlico Market?' says Katie, displaying some frustration.

'They logged the item as stolen to get a crime number.'

'...for an item that wasn't even stolen or missing?'

'Yes, that's right Katie. Mr Carlton-Smyth gave the crime number to his clients who in turn, quite legitimately submitted to their insurance companies for recompense.'

'How is that legitimate? Surely if the client never received the item, they were not financially out of pocket.'

'That is where Mr Carlton-Smyth was clever. After the item had been found and Carlton-Smyth had negotiated an agreed price, the client arranged a bank transfer direct to the vendor and the object d'art was released. You have to remember Katie, these items were all very expensive. Carlton-Smyth didn't have the financial means to provide a bridging loan for the duration of the item leaving the vendor and arriving with the client.'

'Oh I see,' says Katie. 'The client needed a crime number to make a claim on the expensive item they did not receive, but had paid for in advance.'

'Yes, that is right,' says Laura.

'Also, by submitting payment direct to the vendor, it limited suspicion towards Mr Carlton-Smyth,' adds Katie.

'Exactly. As I say, Mr Carlton-Smyth was clever.'

'Notwithstanding, he had the police on his side too,' says Katie.

'Well yes, but these were not police, they were criminals,' says Laura, quick to point out that there is a huge difference.

'My goodness. So where are the objects now? I understand this crime ring, so to speak, had been going on for sometime.'

'You'd be right to expect a whole host of objects lying low somewhere, at least until the missing piece had been forgotten.'

'Yes I would. In a lock-up somewhere,' adds Katie, though going by Laura's expression she quickly realises that the idea of a lock-up might not be what Laura had in mind.

'No. Even before the items were logged with *Art and Antiques Unit* within the Metropolitan Police by DS Trait, they were sold on. Otherwise Mr Carlton-Smyth would be selling stolen goods.'

'They were stolen goods. He stole them.'

'Yes, but when he sold them, they were not officially logged as such,' replies Laura smiling as she waits for Katie to fully grasp the irony.

'So who was actually out of pocket? It was not the vendor, nor the client or either member of the criminal syndicate.'

'Good question Katie.'

'Thank you Laura,' causing Katie to smile, having long since been aware that her own intelligence is no match for Laura's inquisitive journalistic mind.

'Have you ever wondered why your insurance quote leaps up in price year on year?'

'Yes, I do with the car insurance. Every year, I complain.'

'Well, crimes like this don't help.'

'Oh, yes,' says Katie, her eyes wide and shining with excitement. 'The crime is targeting the insurance companies. It is they who are out of pocket.'

'That's right. Out of pocket to feather the nest of Mr Carlton-Smyth, who was until now, a highly respected expert in the art world. Likewise, to feather the nest of DS Trait a young officer who, by all accounts, had a glittering career ahead of her and a Detective Chief Inspector Malcolm Monroe who after a long career with the police, was shortly retiring.'

Katie momentarily turns away from the live feed, back to camera number one and shakes her head in disbelief to deliver a comment to those watching at home. 'You, the tax payer, quite rightly expect these members of authority to be fighting and preventing crime, not creating it.'

'It does leave a rather unpleasant taste...' adds Laura, breaking off for one moment; pressing her ear piece closer to her ear on hearing instructions from the producer. 'Sorry, Katie, I thought the sentencing was upon us but the judge is not yet ready, we can go on.'

'As I understand it, Laura, this criminal racket, if I may call it that, had been going on for sometime without the merest of suspicion from either *Drakes* the Auctioneers or the Metropolitan Police. So what, in the end, was their undoing?'

'The straw that broke the camel's back, upsetting the cogs in the wheel of this finely tuned heist, causing it to come off its tracks to crash and burn, was perhaps the smallest of all the items they had handled. It was a miniature painting from the seventeenth century that, apparently, had its own rumoured history; its own battles and innocence to prove.'

'Was this item destined for the chop so to speak? Was it destined to be sold elsewhere?'

'Indeed it was. Except this piece was more stoic; swathed in its own complexities. From which, unexpected scenarios quickly gathered momentum leading to a whole host of criminal dealings beyond the initial crime. The three of them, it would seem, found themselves caught in something much bigger than the sum of their own parts, which ultimately burst the bubble of their united front.'

'What happened? What actually unmasked them?'

'It seems, given the evidence heard in court this week, that DS Trait, DCI Monroe and Carlton-Smyth, were the architects of their own undoing. Which, I might add, was not from greed or by over playing their hand as you'd expect, but from DCI Monroe denouncing DS Trait, after the unprecedented interjection of this final piece of art; selling his partner in crime down the river.'

'An unorthodox move from a gang member to divert attention from himself and throw others to the hounds?'

'Yes, Katie. Very much so. DCI Monroe could see the writing on the wall and seized an opportunity to disassociate himself from the criminal gang which resulted in their unlawful enterprise imploding before their very eyes.'

'So was this other crime an integral part of exposing their criminal enterprise?' asks Katie.

'On the one hand yes, because it panicked DCI Monroe but on the other hand no. These crimes committed by DCI Monroe, DS Trait and Mr Carlton-Smyth are independent of those surrounding the miniature painting; which has its own story to tell.'

'When can we expect to hear about this other crime, the one with the miniature painting that aided their downfall?' asks Katie.

'So far, no charges have been brought against the perpetrators. They are currently, and may well remain, free of all charges.'

'Why might that be?'

'A whole host of reasons. No one is forced to bring charges. It's the victim's choice as to whether they wish to seek justice. Though given the high profile of this crime to which it is attached, I am quite confident that pressure is being put on those involved to press charges.'

'Either way, the miniature painting will always be remembered as the heist that outsmarted the heist,' says Katie.

'Yes, that does seem to be the case.'

'I can just see Hollywood producers chomping at the bit for this one,' says Katie broadening her grin as she ad libs her way along a path of misplaced enthusiasm. 'Script writers, you might want to get pen to paper...' curtailing her spiel in a flash on seeing the floor manager's determined gesture for her to wrap up this cameo. A notion confirmed on seeing Laura's disgruntled expression for belittling the seriousness of this crime in underestimating the diligence needed to unravel the complexities from the court hearing.

'So there we have it,' says Katie with a sigh, doing her best to ignore the rather dense atmosphere she has created. 'Thank you to Laura Teleosky, our Home

Correspondent, who will update us with details of sentencing throughout the course of the day. Now, moving on to today's other news...'

Sarah Henderson, still leaning against the door frame, fixates her stare to the screen. One by one the profile pictures of Trait, Monroe and Carlton-Smyth disappear replaced with the next pressing news headline. Trevor turns to Sarah and smiles; neither knowing quite what to say. Sarah can feel herself momentarily wrapped up again in the chaos; revisiting the hurt she felt from Monroe's tricks. It was over a year since she'd learnt that her new role as DC was a sham; that she was nothing more than a pawn waiting in the wings to be used in Monroe's game of deception. Yet to this day, she is still embarrassed by the notion of having thought she'd won that role on merit and thinking her potential had at last been noted and fast tracked. She often wonders what tasks she might have been given in their sordid enterprise, if after her probation period, the moment arose for Monroe to bring her out from the shadows. Although she does draw some satisfaction from knowing that without her pertinacious persistences for facts, causing her to visit Mr Dowling at his home after a late lunch and delaying the miniature portrait from finding its way into DS Trait's possession - Jameela may never have married the man she loved. A thought that always makes Henderson smile with a sigh of contentment.

'Oh well,' says Trevor as Sarah straightens up from leaning on the door frame. 'I'm sorry it didn't work out for you as a copper Sarah. Still, it's good to have you back here.'

'Thank you, that is sweet of you,' replies Sarah, knowing that it's taken a good deal of soul searching before having the courage to approach *The British Archives* to ask to be reinstated into the research department. The phone in her pocket vibrates and without hesitation she rushes to answer the call.

'Hello Peter. I didn't need to find a Guardian, I caught the lovely Laura on the lunchtime news. Was I so rubbish at being a detective?'

'Well to be honest...'

'...I don't want you to be honest, Peter. I want you to tell me what I want to hear.'

'Well in that case. You make for a blooming terrific researcher.'

'Thank you.'

'I've been telling you for months it's your forte and here you are, back where you belong.
Stick to that and you will be fine.'

'I've done no research today. In fact, it seems it's my turn to be wasting tax payers' money. What are you doing?' asks Sarah.

'Just standing in front of the fridge. I can't decide

what to have for lunch.'

'Perhaps, pâté? You like pâté.'

'Yes, good idea. Are you still coming to dinner on Thursday?'

'Yes, but I'm not comfortable with carrying on where Carlton-Smyth left off. Perhaps we should wait a while.'

'Are you serious?'

'We should never have looked inside Carlton-Smyth's property. It wasn't our place to do that. Kassri gave me that bag to return safely to its owner. He wasn't expecting me to take advantage of the situation that presented itself.'

'If you don't mind Sarah, I'd prefer you didn't use Kassri as a yard stick to gauge what is moral or immoral otherwise, we shall be stooping very low.'

'Okay, but I feel so guilty for copying all Carlton-Smyth's contacts from that little black book before handing his bag into the police. It sounded fine when you suggested it but now, not so much.'

'Come on. A man has to make a living and Cedric Carlton-Smyth won't need any of those contacts in Wormwood Scrubs or the like.'

·'You've changed Mr Dowling. Are you turning into Al Capone?'

'Everything will be above board,' replies Peter. 'We just need contacts.'

'It will definitely be above board, you can be sure of that.'

'That's settled then. Dinner on Thursday and we shall choose our first client.'

'A client that we will select with the greatest of scrutiny,' adds Sarah.

'Maybe you'd like to go back to work now and do something.'

'Cheeky! Remember I was once DC Henderson, Metropolitan Police, a figure of authority. I had a badge and everything.'

'Erm...is that so...?'

The end.

About The Author

After the success of Michelle Hockley's debut novel, *Before Spring Came Summer*, her second, *For The Sake Of Art* is a validation of her intelligent crafting and directing; along with a musical aptitude and a love for language.

Following the height of a career in Television and performing in London's West End, Michelle read History at Durham University, where her talent for analysis and an investigative prowess took centre stage; leading her to high profile research positions at The National Archives and Historic Royal Palaces where her thesis; *The Escape of Charles I from Hampton Court Palace in 1647*, was published.

Evident in her prose is an established fusion of these incredible talents; combining her musicality and an honesty in her casting.

It has been said of her writing that, 'you won't only get a story, you will also get a moment,' a notion that couldn't be more accurate in her latest offering, *For The Sake Of Art*.